What Kids Say About Carole Marsh Mysteries . . .

I love the real locations! Reading the book always makes me want to go and visit them all on our next family vacation. My Mom says maybe, but I can't wait!

One day, I want to be a real kid in one of Ms. Marsh's mystery books. I think it would be fun, and I think I am a real character anyway. I filled out the application and sent it in and am keeping my fingers crossed!

History was not my favorite subject till I starting reading Carole Marsh Mysteries. Ms. Marsh really brings history to life. Also, she leaves room for the scary and fun.

I think Christina is so smart and brave. She is lucky to be in the mystery books because she gets to go to a lot of places. I always wonder just how much of the book is true and what is made up. Trying to figure that out is fun!

Grant is cool and funny! He makes me laugh a lot!!

I like that there are boys and girls in the story of different ages. Some mysteries I outgrow, but I can always find a favorite character to identify with in these books.

They are scary, but not too scary. They are funny. I learn a lot.
There is always food which makes me hungry. I feel like I am there.

What Adults Say About Carole Marsh Mysteries . . .

I think kids love these books because they have such a wealth of detail.
I know I learn a lot reading them! It's an engaging way to look at the
history of any place or event. I always say I'm only going to read one
chapter to the kids, but that never happens—it's always two or three, at
least! —Librarian

Reading the mystery and going on the field trip—Scavenger Hunt in
hand—was the most fun our class ever had! It really brought the place
and its history to life. They loved the real kids characters and all the
humor. I loved seeing them learn that reading is an experience to
enjoy! —4th grade teacher

Carole Marsh is really on to something with these unique mysteries.
They are so clever; kids want to read them all. The Teacher's Guides
are chock full of activities, recipes, and additional fascinating
information. My kids thought I was an expert on the subject—and
with this tool, I felt like it! —3rd grade teacher

My students loved writing their own Real Kids/Real Places mystery
book! Ms. Marsh's reproducible guidelines are a real jewel. They
learned about copyright and more & ended up with their own book
they were so proud of! —Reading/Writing Teacher

The Mystery on the
UNDERGROUND
RAILROAD

CAROLE MARSH MYSTERIES™

WITHDRAWN

by
Carole Marsh

Carole Marsh Mysteries™ and its skull colophon are the property of Carole Marsh and Gallopade International.

Published by Gallopade International/Carole Marsh Books. Printed in the United States of America.

Editorial Assistant: Margaret S. Ross

Cover Photo Illustration: Michelle Winkleman; Cover design: Vicki DeJoy; Editor: Chad Beard; Graphic Design: Steve St. Laurent; Layout and footer design: Lynette Rowe; Photography: Michael Boylan.
Picture Credits:

The publisher would like to thank the following for their kind permission to reproduce the cover photographs.
© **Nicholas Benton** *Barn*
© **Cindy England** *Antique Quilt*
© **Roxana Gonzalez/Dreamstime** *Vintage Paper*
© **Jon McIntosh** *Antique Lock*

Gallopade International is introducing SAT words that kids need to know in each new book that we publish. The SAT words are bold in the story. Look for this special logo beside each word in the glossary. Happy Learning!

Gallopade is proud to be a member and supporter of these educational organizations and associations:

American Booksellers Association
American Library Association
International Reading Association
National Association for Gifted Children
The National School Supply and Equipment Association
The National Council for the Social Studies
Museum Store Association
Association of Partners for Public Lands

This book is dedicated to the encouragers in my life.

– MR

This book is a complete work of fiction. All events are fictionalized, and although the first names of real children are used, their characterization in this book is fiction.

For additional information on Carole Marsh Mysteries, visit:
www.carolemarshmysteries.com

Imagine . . . only a dolly for a friend.

20 YEARS AGO ...

As a mother and an author, one of the fondest periods of my life was when I decided to write mystery books for children. At this time (1979) kids were pretty much glued to the TV, something parents and teachers complained about the way they do about video games today.

I decided to set each mystery in a real place—a place kids could go and visit for themselves after reading the book. And I also used real children as characters. Usually a couple of my own children served as characters, and I had no trouble recruiting kids from the book's location to also be characters.

Also, I wanted all the kids—boys and girls of all ages—to participate in solving the mystery. And, I wanted kids to learn something as they read. Something about the history of the location. And I wanted the stories to be funny.

That formula of real+scary+smart+fun served me well. The kids and I had a great time visiting each site and many of the events in the stories actually came out of our experiences there. (For example, we really did travel along Harriet Tubman's route from Maryland to Philadelphia!)

I love getting letters from teachers and parents who say they read the book with their class or child, then visited the historic site and saw all the places in the mystery for themselves. What's so great about that? What's great is that you and your children have an experience that bonds you together forever. Something you shared. Something you both cared about at the time. Something that crossed all age levels—a good story, a good scare, a good laugh!

20 years later,

Carole Marsh

Christina Yother

Grant Yother

Clair Coffer

Miles Coffer

ABOUT THE CHARACTERS

Christina Yother, 9, from Peachtree City, Georgia

Grant Yother, 7, from Peachtree City, Georgia
Christina's brother

Clair Coffer as Harriet "Atty," 13, from Baltimore, Maryland is the daughter of a Gallopade International graphic artist.

Miles Coffer as Thaddeus "Duce," 11, Atty's brother, is the son of a Gallopade International graphic artist.

Many of the places featured in the book actually exist and are worth a visit! Perhaps you could read the book and see some of the places the kids visited during their mysterious adventure!

TITLES IN THE REAL KIDS REAL PLACES SERIES

Books and Teacher's Guides are available at booksellers, libraries, school supply stores, museums, and many other locations!

For a complete selection of great Carole Marsh Mysteries, visit www.carolemarshmysteries.com!

CONTENTS

1 YOU HAVE MYSTERY MAIL

Christina was doing a stellar job helping her Grandmother Mimi when the **intriguing** e-mail invitation arrived. Grant was also being a big help by stuffing the giant pile of newspaper clippings, scattered across Mimi's desk, back into the correct color-coded folders.

Christina Yother, 9, a fourth-grader in Peachtree City, Georgia, her brother Grant, 7, and Mimi stood staring at the new message on Mimi's office computer screen. Suddenly, Mimi's 122 unread e-mails were completely forgotten.

Dear Aunt Mimi:
    The National Park Service, The National Museum of American History, Professor William B. Still and I invite

An E-mail
Invitation

To Where?

Christina and Grant to ride the *Freedom Road*
on the U.R.R. We'll be pulling into Baltimore
next Tuesday to pick up four passengers.
We'll **rendezvous** with you and the other
VIPs in Philly for the formal ribbon cutting
on the Fourth of July.
Priscilla :-)
Assistant Curator

Next Tuesday? The notice was short but Christina
knew that didn't really matter to her Grandmother Mimi.
She was not like most grandmothers. She wasn't really like
a grandmother at all. She had blond hair, wore trendy
clothes, was CEO of her own company, and traveled all
around the country!

Mimi tapped the message on the screen with her
pink fingernail as she thought about it. "Hmmm," she said.
"This just needs some organization and action, but what an
adventure this could be!" Mimi typed a reply, then reached
for her cell phone.

Christina was nearly bursting with questions.
"Mimi, is this a good time to ask questions?"

"You bet!" said Mimi, stroking her granddaughter's
soft, chestnut-colored hair. "I always have time for

To Where?

from Cousin
Priscilla

questions!"

But Christina shocked her grandmother by reeling out a string of questions: "Why does the e-mail say National Museum of American History? Is this the same U.R.R. we learned about in school? Did Cousin Priscilla get a new job? Isn't that museum in Washington, DC? What exactly is the *Freedom Road*? Does this mean we'll all be together for a Philadelphia Fourth of July celebration? Are you a VIP?"

"Whoa! Good questions!" said Mimi. "Let's start at the end and work our way forward. It's important to remember that everyone we meet is a very important person (VIP) and should be treated with courtesy and respect. Yes, this means we will all be in Philadelphia for the Fourth of July. So much of America's history happened there that it's one of my favorite places to be!"

Mimi took a deep breath and continued answering Christina's many questions. "*Freedom Road* is a new mobile American History museum. Priscilla is still a wonderful fourth grade history teacher and marathoner! She has worked at the museum every summer since she was in high school. Papa and I have been helping with the research for this new museum-on-wheels, so we've been invited to the ribbon-cutting for *Freedom Road's* official Grand Opening."

We're Going On A Trip!

The Fourth In Philly!

Mimi paused for another breath and added, "By the way, congratulations on remembering! It *is* the very same U.R.R. you learned about in school.

Mimi looked down at Grant who was still staring at the screen with a perplexed expression. He looked serious. "Everything okay, Grant?" asked Mimi.

Perched on the edge of her office chair, with his legs swinging high above the floor, Grant looked very small. His blue eyes seemed the biggest part of him. He looked up. "Well for one thing, I haven't studied U.R.R. or *urrrrr*. Or however you say it! Is it like *grrrr*? I happen to know a lot about *grrrr*. *Grrrr* could be a bear or an angry dog. Papa told me that I'm supposed to remain as 'still as a statue' if I hear *that* sound. I still have a question. It might sound dumb, but we haven't covered all the things in my grade that Christina knows."

"What's that?" asked Mimi. "There are no dumb questions, you know."

Grant quietly asked, "Mimi, what *is* U.R.R.?"

His grandmother squeezed his small tense shoulder and smiled. "Grant, that's a wonderful question! It stands for the Underground Railroad. The Underground Railroad didn't have railroad cars or rails. It had people. It was a top secret organization of people, both black and white,

The Fourth
In Philly!

What Is The
U.R.R.?

who risked their lives to help slaves escape from Southern states, where slavery was allowed, to freedom in the North."

Since Grant still looked confused, Mimi continued her explanation. "Some people say that the Underground Railroad really began in the 1700s when slaves were brought to America from Africa. Other people say it began about 1830 when it got an official name. The railroad was spoken of in hopeful whispers and hidden in songs that were sung across the plantations. The organization had its own secret language, clues, and codes. Even today the story of the slaves' escape to freedom is filled with myths and mystery."

Grant still looked concerned. Mimi asked, "Are you still worried about something?"

Grant looked at this grandmother thoughtfully. "If we're going to be traveling under the ground, will Priscilla bring the flashlights, or should we each bring our own?"

What Is The U.R.R.?

A Network Of People

2 PORCH SWING THINGS

It had been another busy day. Mimi stepped out on her wide, front porch, kicked off her shoes, and plopped down into her favorite white, wicker rocking chair. She planned to spend a few quiet minutes rocking, reading her mail, listening to the birds sound their evening chirps, and watching the golden glow of the summer sun setting over her two big magnolia trees laden with white, fragrant, blossoms the size of dinner plates.

She got to enjoy that peaceful experience for about 45 wonderful seconds before being interrupted. A car pulled into her driveway and family poured out. "Mimi! Mimi!" shouted Grant and Christina. "Want to go for a swim? It's not dark yet!"

"Thank you, but not right now, tadpoles," answered Mimi. "You are welcome to sit here with me. We can talk

Time To Relax

Maybe Not!

a little bit about your trip to Baltimore and the Underground Railroad."

They both climbed into the chair beside her.

"Ok, Mimi," answered Christina, "but I have to tell you that talking is usually not nearly as much fun as swimming."

"Did I ever tell you two that if Papa and I had been living 150 years ago, we would have been abolitionists?" Mimi asked.

"Is that a good thing or a bad thing?" asked Grant.

"Why are you telling us now? Is someone going to ask us about this in Baltimore on Tuesday?" asked Christina.

"Good questions," Mimi answered. "I'm telling you now so you'll remember that an abolitionist was a person who believed slavery was wrong and should be ended."

"Ok, but why is this important for our trip, Mimi?" Christina asked again.

"It's important, Christina, because the Civil War and the Underground Railroad were such turning points in America's history. Before your trip begins, you are going to need to know how the slavery story *began* in America," Mimi said.

"Is this a lesson or a story?" Christina asked.

Maybe Not!   Story With
                                                         A Lesson

Mimi gave them both a big squeeze, until they squealed, and said, "It's a story *with* a lesson! Don't worry. I'll give you the short version."

Mimi began: "In 1719, 600 Africans were taken against their will and brought to America and sold as slaves to work on plantations–large farms–in the South. That was the beginning of more than 100 years of slavery in America."

"The life of a plantation slave was very difficult," she continued. "Field hands–including children–worked as long as 15 hours a day. Their homes were often small crowded huts or shacks. Slaves were usually given very little food and clothing from their owners."

Mimi sighed. "Slaves could be sold whenever their owners chose to do so. Men, women, and children could be taken from their families and separated at any time. Slaves were placed on an auction block to be sold to the highest bidder. Buyers were only interested in the strongest slaves because they could do the most heavy work in the fields. Family members could be sold to different owners and perhaps never see one another again."

"Long days, hard work, disease, and bad weather often made plantation life one of misery. The crops most often grown on plantations were rice, cotton, and tobacco.

Story With
A Lesson

Story With
A Lesson

Even the youngest slave children had to work in the fields–dawn to dusk!"

"The Underground Railroad was a way for slaves to escape this misery and hopefully have a better life," Mimi concluded.

"When did slavery end, Mimi?" asked Christina.

"Not for a very long time," Mimi replied. "In America, it ended in 1863. That's when the Emancipation Proclamation was issued by U.S. President Abraham Lincoln."

"Slavery was awful!" said Christina. "I'm glad we don't have slaves today."

"Me too!" said Grant.

Mimi looked sad. "In some places in the world, slavery still exists–even today!"

Story With
A Lesson

All About
Slavery!

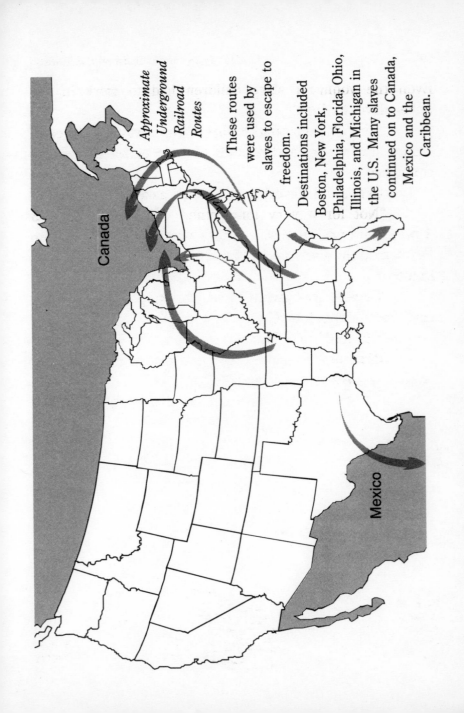

Approximate
Underground
Railroad
Routes

These routes
were used by
slaves to escape to
freedom.
Destinations included
Boston, New York,
Philadelphia, Florida, Ohio,
Illinois, and Michigan in
the U.S. Many slaves
continued on to Canada,
Mexico and the
Caribbean.

Canada

Mexico

3 BALTIMORE OR BUST

Tuesday morning, Uncle Michael, Christina, Grant, and Mimi raced toward Hartsfield International Airport, the busiest in the nation, in Atlanta. Papa, their grandfather, was taking them so they didn't have to leave a car and "pay through the nose." He liked to be frugal with his money.

Grant thought of someone paying a parking bill through their nose, and snickered. Papa was always saying things that Grant didn't understand yet. His grandfather had lots and lots of opinions. He had opinions on everything, even opinions. Papa never seemed to run out of things to say.

"In my opinion," Papa suddenly said, "we should stop here and use curbside check-in, so we don't have to pull into the pay parking lot." Grant knew that meant they

To The Atlanta Airport!

To The Atlanta Airport!

were going to stop the car right now, and everyone needed to pile out as quickly as possible. Papa wanted to be out of there before the policeman walking their way could tell him to "Move along, please, sir!" or "You can't park here!" Something about the policeman saying that always made Papa grumble and even say *grrrrr*!

Mimi had suggested that they all fly to Baltimore together and asked Papa to see about getting a refund on their tickets to Philadelphia. He said, "By the time they charge us for changes, there won't be any refund at all. That's just throwing good money after bad!" Grant had no idea why the tickets to Philadelphia were paid for with bad money. And how did his grandfather even know the difference between good money and bad money?

In the end Mimi worked it all out. She talked Uncle Michael into making his business trip to New York with a short stop in Baltimore. Papa like their plan because they could "kill two birds with . . ." Everyone finished that opinion for him, shouting, "With one stone!" Then they all laughed. Everyone knew that it was one of Papa's all-time favorite sayings.

Mimi was the first one out of the car. She left Papa grumbling about "paying through the nose" for airline tickets and being accused of "parking" when anyone could

At The Atlanta
Airport

Dropping
Off!

clearly see that he was only "pausing." He agreed to circle the airport once and pick Mimi up in five minutes.

Mimi and Christina ran to buy magazines, peanut butter crackers, Junior Mints, and other essential airline survival stuff. After a lot of slobbery hugs and kisses (Grant's opinion), Mimi slipped a bright red plastic whistle on a red, white and blue shoelace around his neck. "If you need me just whistle and I'll come running," she whispered in Grant's ear. "I'll see you in Philly on the fourth!"

Usually it was Uncle Michael who gave him weird, neat stuff that "might come in handy." Grant still had the small pen flashlight, safely tucked into his backpack, that Uncle Michael had given him a few months ago.

"Listen to your cousin Priscilla and take good care of Grant," Mimi told Christina, giving her a big hug and slipping extra money into her pocket, just in case of "emergencies."

"You can count on me," Christina said in a confident voice. "You better hurry, Mimi, or Papa will be having words with another airport policeman!" Christina was pretending to be very grownup and brave. Mimi was pretending not to notice that she was pretending.

"All aboard for Baltimore, Maryland and the Underground Railroad!" boomed Uncle Michael in his best

Dropping Off!

All Aboard!

Papa voice.

"Shhh!   Uncle Michael!"   Grant whispered. "Our destination is supposed to be top secret!"

4 HE TAKES THE CAKE

It was a great flight. Both Grant and Christina had window seats and got a good aerial look at several of Washington, D.C.'s famous landmarks. "That's the Pentagon coming up now," the captain told them. "The Washington Monument and the U.S. Capitol will be coming up on our port side in about eight seconds," he added. "Did any of you happen to know that without the generosity of the state of Maryland, there wouldn't even be a Washington, D.C.? In 1791, Maryland donated the land to the new nation for its capital."

The captain continued, "Maryland is the birthplace of the famous and the infamous. We're proud to be the birth state of the most famous conductor on the Underground Railroad, Harriet Tubman. She was born here in 1821. That's all for now, folks! There's an airport

Flying To
Baltimore

Ready To
Land

coming up, so I'd better get back to work!"

A few minutes later, they bumped down in Baltimore. The engines whined as the plane slowed to taxi in from the end of the runway. In a few minutes, while they waited to be towed the last few feet, the captain announced, "Welcome! Baltimore's weather is typical for July. It's sunny, hot, and humid. Wherever your travels take you, please stay alert. Stay safe."

That's almost sounds like a warning, Christina thought to herself. And why was he talking about the Underground Railroad?

Soon they were in the terminal, and there stood their cousin Priscilla holding a sign with their names on it. Uncle Michael gave Priscilla a kiss on the cheek, kissed his niece and nephew, and dashed off to make his flight to New York. "They're all yours Priscilla!" he called over his shoulder. As they watched, he disappeared into the crowd.

Priscilla spent a lot of time with kids, so she didn't do any of that usual hugging and kissing and "look how big they've grown" and all that other meeting and greeting stuff. What she did say was music to their ears. "Anybody hungry?" she asked.

Grant tried out one of Papa's famous sayings. In his deepest voice he said, "Priscilla, I'm so hungry that my

Ready To Land

Priscilla!

stomach thinks my throat's been cut!"

"Yuck, that's disgusting!" Christina scolded him. "Be polite."

"Well it wouldn't be very polite for me to die of starvation in the airport," Grant said. "Does anyone happen to have a spare cookie in their bag?"

Priscilla wisely ignored the conversation and helped them gather up their suitcases and backpacks.

"Where are Professor Still and his grandchildren?" asked Christina shyly. Mimi had told her that Harriet was very smart, had a beautiful singing voice, and played on the boys soccer team. I just hope she doesn't think she can tell me what to do just because she's older than me or because her grandfather is Priscilla's boss at the museum, Christina thought.

"We have a wonderful surprise for you!" Priscilla told them. "We're meeting them at the City Light's Seafood Restaurant at the Inner Harbor. It's been one of my favorite places to eat since I was about your age, Grant. It also has one of the best views in the entire city."

"Wow!" Grant blurted. "Since you were my age? That must be a really, really long time ago!"

Christina tried to stop her brother's chatter by stepping on his toes. He didn't take the hint. Instead he

Priscilla!

To Inner Harbor

shouted, "Hey, you stepped on my toes!"

"I had to stop you!" Christina whispered. "It's considered rude to tell a grown woman that she's old. Especially when she's barely 25! Really, Grant!"

"I don't get it," grumbled Grant, as he examined the toe of his new shoe for signs of damage. "But I'd rather eat than think anyway. If we are going to a seafood restaurant, I'll order a hamburger and French fries. Yum!"

"I've placed the order, Grant. You're getting a golden brown patty of Maryland's most famous cake," Priscilla told him.

Grant grinned. "Fine with me! I love cake! Is it chocolate?"

"It's a *crab* cake," said Priscilla. It comes with hush puppies and coleslaw. Have you ever eaten fresh, steamed oysters?"

Christina rolled her eyes and sighed. "Forget it, Priscilla. Once when Mimi put one on his plate, Grant said he couldn't eat anything that reminded him of a dinosaur booger!"

Professor Still walked up to their table, two kids trailing behind. He looked a little older than Papa. He had

To Inner
Harbor

Time To Eat!

intelligent brown eyes that twinkled behind his wire-rimmed glasses. The top of his shiny, chocolate brown head was surrounded by a short, curly white halo of hair.

He looks a king or an angel, Christina thought. And when he spoke, Professor Still's voice reminded her of the actor James Earl Jones. It was definitely a voice made for preaching or keeping college students from nodding off in class.

"Welcome!" he boomed as he stepped forward to give Christina a firm hand shake. He looked Christina right in the eyes and slowly smiled. Mimi always said that you could "take a person's measure by how they shook your hand." Christina remembered Mimi telling her that 'measure' was an impression or feeling. Was the person honest and kind or maybe a little sneaky and mean?

Suddenly remembering her manners, Christina thanked him for the invitation. He leaned closer and listened carefully to every word she said. She wondered if the professor was taking her measure, too. Christina was totally surprised by his next remark.

"Priscilla tells me that you and Grant are good people to have along if an adventure might include danger."

Is he teasing, Christina wondered. Is this a test? Christina was soon to replay that moment in her mind over

Time To Eat!

Meet Professor Still!

and over again.

Abruptly changing the mood, Professor Still declared, "Enough of that now! We are here to join you for dinner. Atty and Duce insist they are starving. We will join you and order *post-haste*."

All the fun ended for Grant when the waiter brought him something that looked like a giant fish burger but without the cheese or bun. Christina noticed the look on his face.

"Maybe I should have ordered the post-haste," he said forlornly.

Duce learned over and spoke quietly to Grant. "Take a bite. It's really delicious."

Grant put a small bite in his mouth and chewed. His blue eyes widened in pleasant surprise. Duce was right. It *was* delicious. "Who would have thunk it!" Grant said.

Meet Professor
Still!

Yum! Crab
Cakes

5 STILL WATERS RUN DEEP

"Oh, excuse me," said Professor Still, who had been having a whispered conversation with Priscilla. "Allow me to introduce you to two fellow adventurers, my grandchildren. This is the lovely Harriet, 13, and the charming Thaddeus, 11. For some reason that I absolutely do not understand, they prefer to be called Atty and Duce."

"Great to finally meet you! We've heard your cousin and grandmother talk about you for so long that we feel we already know you," said Atty. She turned to her grandfather and teased him a motherly voice. "Let's eat *and* talk, Grandpa Will."

Duce turned to Grant and Christina explaining, "Sometimes he forgets to eat when he's talking about any of his favorite subjects: the Underground Railroad, *Freedom Road,* or anything to do with American history." Duce

Yum! Crab
Cakes

Meet Atty
And Duce

grinned hugely and added, "I personally find it impossible to understand anybody forgetting to eat!"

As if on cue, Professor Still began telling them the Still family's own Underground Railroad story.

"My great-great-great-grandfather's name was also William Still. He was born a slave in 1821. A slave had no rights and was considered the property of his owner. At one time, in the southern United States, slavery was not against man's law. It has always been against God's law. I believe that God planted in the heart of every person the need to be free. This is so important that brave people have *always* been willing to face death in order to gain freedom. That belief is the reason for the Underground Railroad."

Professor Still continued his tale, not noticing his dinner had grown cold on his plate. Christina felt like she was holding her breath and straining to catch every word. Mimi was big on oral history, and Christina thought this one sounded fascinating.

"The first William Still escaped slavery and settled in Philadelphia in 1844. He was the first black member of the Philadelphia Anti-Slavery Society. He made speeches, raised money, and faced daily dangers such as being captured by bounty hunters who were paid big rewards to

Meet Atty And
Duce

Some Oral
History

capture escaped slaves and send them back to the South or put them in jail."

Professor Still sighed, then continued with his story. "He was what was known as a 'conductor' on the Underground Railroad. A conductor was a person who volunteered to go into the South and lead slaves to safety in the North. Conductors took their 'passengers' (other code words included packages, freight, and dry goods) from one 'station' to the next. Naturally, secret organizations don't keep detailed records but it's estimated that by 1850 nearly 3,000 people worked on the Underground Railroad. They helped more than 50,000 slaves escape!"

Christina looked around at the others. Usually, she thought, kids didn't much like to sit around listening to long tales of history but she could tell from their wide eyes that all of the kids–including her–were captivated by Professor Still's family story. It was not history that she was very familiar with. She wondered why she had not studied all this in school!

The professor continued, "William Still was also our family's first historian. Not only was he *making* history, he was also *recording* it for future generations. For nearly 30 years, he wrote the escape stories and kept them safely

Some Oral
History

Recording
History

hidden. In 1872, after slavery was abolished, he published a book called *Underground Railroad Records*."

"What few people know is that the most exciting and priceless stories never made it into the published book. But they can still be found in a secret place!"

"Where, Professor Still?" Christina exclaimed. "Where are they now?"

"William Still's unpublished journal is part of the *Freedom Road's* Underground Railroad exhibit. Our family is loaning it to the museum. It will rest in a place of honor, as will a freedom quilt that donated by the family of Harriet Tubman."

Professor Still looked out the restaurant's big window at the harbor view below. Turning to Atty he said, "We are surrounded by history! Look over there, young Atty. See the ship at the dock? Tell our guests about it. They may find it interesting!"

Atty changed her voice to sound like a tour guide on a San Francisco trolley car. Everyone giggled.

"Haaarumph! Over there on our starboard side, ladies and gentlemen, we see the *USS Constellation*. By the way, starboard is the right side if we have any landlubbers with us today! It's a sailing vessel that was launched in Baltimore in 1797. It was the first United States Navy

Recording
History

The USS
Constellation

vessel to capture an enemy warship."

In a fake whisper she said to Christina. "What can I say–there's history in my blood! If we have time after touring *Freedom Road*, and if you're not too tired of fish and seafood, we can walk *over there*." She pointed past the *Constellation*, and Christina saw the entrance to the Baltimore Aquarium. Duce and Christina groaned loudly to show their appreciation for her attempt at humor.

"I understand completely!" Christina told her. "I, too, have history–and mystery–flowing through my veins! It must be in our genes."

"Must get crowded in there sometimes," Grant said with a grin.

"Speaking of *Freedom Road*," said Priscilla as she reached into her backpack and pulled out brightly colored packages, "we have something for each of you as a memory of this trip."

Each package contained a soft white T-shirt and a bright red baseball cap. Each shirt had the child's name and *Freedom Road Staff* embroidered over the pocket in bright blue.

Quickly pulling his new shirt over his head, Grant saluted and announced to the entire restaurant, "Grant reporting for duty! Point me toward my vessel–the *USS*

The USS
Constellation

To Freedom
Road!

Freedom Road!"

"Aye, Aye, Grant! Follow me," answered Priscilla.

To Freedom Road!

6 THE BIG BLUE BUS

The first thing that came to Christina's mind as she turned the corner and saw the *Freedom Road* for the first time was–major country music star! It was an awesome sight. The mobile museum, like a very large and swanky bookmobile, was painted metallic blue and decorated with a spray of 50 glistening red and white stars.

Christina could imagine the oversized bus flying down the highway on its tour, with people gasping and pointing to it, asking, "What was *that?*" At every stop on the tour, people would line up to see the amazing interactive exhibits inside and learn about the history of the famous Underground Railroad.

"I think we should rename this mobile museum *On The Road,*" Christina told the others. "That's a much better name for a country music star's personal vehicle." Waving

To freedom Road!

An Awesome Sight

her arm above her head, she said in her most royal sounding voice, "From now on you will be officially known by cool kids everywhere and–maybe Reba McIntyre–as *The Road.*"

Grant rushed to the side of the vehicle, gave it a little tap and grinned at his sister.

"What was that about Grant?" she asked him suspiciously. "What are you doing?"

"Can't you guess?" Grant replied. "Watch me! I'll do it again!" After repeating the tapping, he looked at her expectantly. "Got it yet?" he asked.

A light went on for Christina. He is getting smarter all the time, Christina thought. I'll soon have to stay on my toes around him. But he hasn't put one over on me yet!

"Of course, I got it, Grant. You didn't fool me. You were 'Hitting The Road!'" she said. Christina used her slightly bored voice.

"No you didn't!" Grant chirped happily as he twirled and jumped around her. "No you didn't! You didn't get it. I got you. I got yoooooo!"

Priscilla told them that the *Road's* air horn and speaker system were programmed to play 30 patriotic melodies. In honor of the Underground Railroad exhibit, they had also added a wide selection of folk songs and

An Awesome
Sight

A Mobile
Museum

hymns from 1800s. Christina remembered Mimi saying that secret codes and messages were often hidden in the words of the songs that slaves sang while they worked.

The roof of the museum had a satellite dish, a field of antennas, and even a global positioning system (GPS). Priscilla said, "The GPS helps keep track of the museum while it's on the road and it could connect us to a directions center if we got lost." Not even country music stars had anything as wonderful as this, Christina thought.

Priscilla greeted the security guard and signed her name on his computer tablet. Next she showed picture ID's and permission letters for all four kids. Museum rules required that the *Road* could never be left alone. It was too valuable. An employee had to stay with it at all times. After they had cleared through the next level of security at the door, the guard would be allowed to leave.

It was just like the movies! There was a computer touch screen close to the door. Professor Still put his hand on the screen, spoke his name and the password for the day. The computer scanned his handprint and finger print. Next it matched his voice to the one recorded on file in Washington, D.C.

After several quiet seconds, a musical computer voice said, *"Welcome back to Freedom Road, Professor Still.*

A Mobile
Museum

A Mobile
Museum

It's been 2 hours and 35 seconds since your last visit. Please remember to watch your step, Professor, as you enter the museum. We hope you and your guests enjoy your time with us today. We see that this is a first visit for Priscilla's cousins, Christina and Grant."

"Grant," Christina teased, "close your mouth or a fly might get in!" Christina was amazed, and Grant was speechless. Grant reached up and put his small hand on the computer screen. This time the musical voice was louder. It said, *"Warning. Unauthorized person attempting access. Please step away from the door! The Freedom Road is not open for visitors at this time. Normal business hours are posted on the door. Please visit us during normal business hours."*

Christina gave him a little tug toward the door as he reached for the screen for the second time.

"Psst! Christina!" Atty called to her. "We're ready to begin our private tour. Come on in." Taking Grant by the hand, Christina stepped inside.

"I'm going to load our gear," Priscilla said, returning outside.

After the heat and sun of the hot summer day, it was a welcome relief–cool, dim, and pleasant on the inside.

Welcome to Freedom Road. Let your museum tour

A Mobile
Museum

Onto
Freedom Road

begin! *Look up to the ceiling! Look to the stars!* The disembodied recorded voice of Professor Still came over the speakers in deep, rich tones. Christina wanted to tell him that he sounded even better than James Earl Jones in *The Lion King* but felt too shy to say so. The lights dimmed even further. As they watched the ceiling, it turned into a clear summer night's sky. Crickets could be heard softly chirping. Christina loved special effects. She wasn't absolutely sure, but they might have even added the sound of a dog barking in the distance and a faraway rumble of an approaching summer storm for their soundtrack. Stars twinkled in the night sky.

The voice continued, *Underground Railroad 'conductors' guided their passengers northward toward freedom using the North Star and the Big Dipper to guide them. Watch closely, and see if you can find the North Star.*

As they watched, one group of stars began glowing brighter than the rest. The North Star began to twinkle. It was beautiful. Everyone found themselves saying "Ooooooohhhhh!" and "Ahhhhhhhhh!" Then they all laughed at themselves.

The ceiling stars dissolved and were replaced by a picture that looked like a weather map on TV. Christina was sure that this map had nothing to do with heat waves,

Onto Freedom
Road

A Summer
Evening

approaching showers, or the jet stream.

While they watched, a map of the United States appeared, covered with a number of wide, red curving arrows. The voice continued, *This unique 'railroad' is reported to have had more than 1,000 'stations' that zigzagged northward along two major routes. One was along the Eastern Seaboard slave states: Florida, Georgia, South Carolina, North Carolina, and Virginia where slaves raced toward the free states of Delaware and Pennsylvania. Escaping slaves from Mississippi, Alabama, Louisiana, Arkansas, Tennessee, Kentucky, Missouri, and Texas moved toward the safety of the free states of Ohio, Michigan, Indiana, and Illinois. Many followed the North Star across the Great Lakes and into Canada.*

The recorded voice droned on, *Many 'conductors' tried to move their 'passengers' up to 20 miles each night. Unfortunately, some nights they traveled less than five. Saturday was the night most escapes happened because slaves owners could not put 'escaped slave' notices in the paper until Monday.*

The lights came on and the kids applauded. Priscilla and Professor Still looked like proud parents at a piano recital.

"That's exactly the kind of response we've been

The U.R.R. Route

Other Goodies!

hoping for!" the professor told them.

"Grandpa Will," said Duce excitedly, "what do you want to show us next? Quilt codes? Computer simulations? Harriet's Story? The Still journal?"

Before the professor could answer, Atty interrupted. "Did you get the bugs worked out of the **virtual** reality headsets, yet? You can practice on us! What do you think Grandpa Will? Please!"

Quilt Codes?

Virtual Reality?

7 HIGH-TECH HISTORY

Professor Still nodded toward the tall, black three-drawer cabinet that stood immediately to his left. He said, "They are in the top drawer, Duce. Help yourself."

Turning to the rest of the kids, he added, "This is our newest model of the VRGG–Virtual Reality Goggle-Gloves. The computer geniuses at the lab in Washington tell me that they will really work this time. Of course, that's exactly what they told me the last four times!

Patting Duce lightly on his shoulder, Professor Still explained, "Duce was brave enough to try out the last version for me a few weeks ago. I'm sorry to report that it was *not* a happy experience. Unfortunately, something was wrong with the goggles. After only a few minutes, Duce became so dizzy that we had to help him to a chair before he fell over!"

Virtual Reality?

Dizzy Duce

"Or threw up!" Duce added, holding his stomach dramatically.

"However," Professor Still said, "The new ones just arrived this morning. If any of you are feeling high-tech today, I'll let you try them out at one of the exhibits. I'd suggest starting with something pretty simple like the quilt exhibit. With luck, if the equipment is working as we expect, you should be able to experience what it was like to be part of a Charleston, South Carolina quilting bee in the early 1820s. If you'll pardon my pun, think of it as an easy way to get 'hands on' experience!"

Duce walked over and pulled the drawer toward him. It was just about level with his head. Stretching a little, Duce felt around in the drawer his grandfather had been talking about. He pulled the odd-looking equipment sets out of the drawer one at a time and carefully handed one to each of his fellow adventurers. They each took a pair of large black gloves and a shiny goggle headset.

At first, Christina decided that the glove material might be made of foil it was so light and thin. The glove material *did* feel like foil. Christina quickly slipped her hand into her right glove and curled her fingers into a tight ball. But after a few quick tests she changed her mind. Christina had expected the glove to make a crackling sound

Dizzy Duce

Gloves &
Headsets!

when she moved her fingers but it didn't. When she examined the bend of each finger, she expected to see wrinkles in the material. Hmmm. Wrong again. It hadn't wrinkled. Foil had been the wrong guess. Each of her gloves was connected to her goggle headset with three long, needle-thin, green wires. Christina tucked her goggle headset under her chin while she put on the other glove.

Since Duce had done this before, he stepped in to help. "Christina," Duce warned, "You'll want to put your goggle headset on *before* your gloves because the wires will get tangled if you don't! I know–I did it wrong the first time."

Christina didn't appreciate Duce acting like a know-it-all and was just about to tell him off. Luckily, Atty noticed the rising tension and she stepped in to make them laugh. "We can get to all that later, Duce," Atty said. "First, let's turn around and look at our reflections in the mirrored wall and see how funny we look!"

They spun around and burst out laughing. "We look like giant insects!" Atty said with a laugh.

She was right, that is exactly what we look like, Christina thought. I've come to Baltimore to become a human fly! She was actually very excited and a little nervous. "Explain what we should expect, please,

Gloves &
Headsets!

Human Flies!

Professor Still," Christina said.

"Delighted to, Christina," Professor Still replied. "This is an experimental three-dimensional virtual reality exhibit system. Many museum curators are limited in how they can help visitors experience history. A quilting exhibit might have a video for you to watch, a simple computer presentation, or they might have a way for you to sew a few stitches. Not here. We do much better than that! We can do high-tech history on the *Freedom Road*."

Professor Still continued his demonstration. "When you stand in the green footprint lights on the floor directly in front of the exhibit and put on your gloves and goggle headset, you'll feel like you actually are part of the quilting bee. You can sew stitches into a virtual quilt. In the simplest terms, you are no longer only an observer. You will become a full participant in history! Perhaps I should say that you'll become a full *virtual* participant. Remember, it feels real, but it's not."

Christina wasn't too sure how she felt about participating in *anything* that had happened in 1820. She said, "Professor Still, what if I don't like it? How do I get out of there? I might find that I don't like quilting. I might get dizzy and fall over like Duce. I'll need an escape hatch."

"It is very simple," Professor Still told her. "You can

Human Flies

Virtual
Quilting

press the red, triangle-shaped OFF button on the outside corner of your headset or simply take it off. Remember, Christina, you won't *really* move even a step. It will just *feel* like you are. Are you kids ready to give it a try?"

"I'll go if everyone else goes, too," Christina offered.

Duce replied, "No way in *virtual* or any other reality am I going to a quilting bee. Forget it."

"Would it be alright if we see the William Still journal and the Tubman quilt first and try our hand at quilting later?" Christina asked.

"Of course," said the professor. "It is just down here on our left. Follow me."

With Grant in the lead, the kids followed Professor Still like a group of ducklings. The Still Journal exhibit was a tinted glass box, about the size of a microwave oven. The bottom was lined with rich red velvet. Nestled in the center was a battered, brown leather journal. The gold stamped lettering looked like it had worn off a hundred years ago.

Christina felt disappointed. It looks so fragile, Christina thought. The corners of the journal were bent and the pages rippled with water damage. Over the years the pages had become as dry and brittle as autumn leaves on the school sidewalks crumbling at a touch. After

Virtual
Quilting

The Still
Journal

hearing Professor Still's wonderful story, she had definitely been expecting something much grander than this poor, battered little book. I am *not* impressed, she decided. She hoped the quilt would be a little more interesting.

Suddenly Priscilla rejoined them and gave Christina a reassuring smile. She pointed out the tattered old quilt hanging in a glass case.

"Priscilla," Christina asked, "what part did quilts and codes play in the Underground Railroad?"

"Quilts were used in the South to let runaway slaves know if a house was safe or not," Priscilla explained. "They were hung on clotheslines or porch banisters. If a quilt had black cloth, a color block, a symbol of a drinking gourd, or the North Star, slaves knew that it was a safe house to go to for help."

Christina's nose nearly touched the display case as she stared at the quilt. After a few moments of concentration, Christina broke into a huge grin. "I see it, Priscilla," Christina crowed. "I think I can break the code!"

All three code symbols were there! Christina ticked them off on her fingers. One of the four boxes in each quilt section was black. Drinking gourds had been carefully stitched into the quilt's pattern. And in the upper right-hand corner of each quilt square Christina saw a star!

The Still Journal

Quilt Codes

What must have gone through the mind of a girl my age, she wondered, who was running for her life, hungry and tired, when she saw this quilt? As if the words had been whispered in her ears, Christina knew the answer! She felt she understood the message of the simple, faded quilt. Welcome. You are safe with us.

Christina usually felt very safe. Of course, she had no way to know that the old journal and quilt would soon involve them all in a dangerous mystery!

Quilt Codes

Message Of Safety

8 Spooky Highway

Christina turned from the quilt exhibit and called out, "Professor Still, Grant and I are ready to go to the 1820 Quilting Bee. Where are the footprints on the floor Grant should use?"

"I do *not* want to go there, Christina," Grant insisted. "I'll try out the VRGG but let's use it with the journal and not the quilt."

"I'll try it, too," added Duce excitedly.

Priscilla carefully took them through the steps. "First, everyone step on a set of green footprints on the floor in front of the exhibit." Each child followed her instructions. Grant's painted footprints were nearly twice as large as his real feet.

"Now, pick a story from the book." Priscilla touched the computer screen next to the journal exhibit. The list of

Let's Go Virtual

Step On The footprints

slaves' names and stories appeared on the screen–just like a book's table of contents.

Reading down the list, Priscilla wrinkled her brow in thought. "Umm. Let's choose the story of someone about your age," she said, and pressed the button on the computer's touch screen that said CLARA, 10, GEORGIA SLAVE.

Christina, Grant, Atty, and Duce adjusted their goggles. Professor Still helped them into their gloves. They were very careful, and no one got their wires tangled.

"Ok, adventurers," Professor Still, began, "Here you go on your journey to the past!"

Grant was standing closest to the computer screen. While he watched, a large, yellow button with flashing red letters appeared. The word on the button said START. Grant watched it flash a few times and reached out and pressed it. He had not intended to press it. The program began to run. As they felt the virtual 'feel' kick in, the totally surprised kids all responded with the same sounds, "AHHHHHHHHHH! OOOOHHHHHHHH!"

Plunk. Christina suddenly became aware that she was outside somewhere in the country, and it was night. She felt the dirt road under her bare feet. She heard the sounds of the night. She knew that they must be miles

Step On The
footprints

The Virtual
feel

from the nearest city. Where was she? Was it *still* July? Why was she so cold? Christina was no longer wearing her jeans, shirt, and sneakers. Instead, she had on a tattered, dirty, shapeless dress that felt like a burlap sack–rough and scratchy. A rope belt was knotted loosely around her waist. Her beautiful silky hair was matted and dirty. The gnawing feeling in her stomach was both fear and hunger. She felt breathless. Had she been running, she wondered?

A cloud that covered the moon moved on. Christina could see a little better. Christina, Grant, Atty, and Duce were on road.

"Pssst, psst, hey you girl, you boy!" came a voice from the darkness at the side of the road. *"Get off dat road. It's moon bright tonight and the slave catchers are out fer sure. Come over here now!"*

All did as they were told and found themselves crouched and trembling next to a tiny black girl. She was dressed like they were and clutched a burlap sack in her hand.

"I be Clara," she told them. *"I made a quilt with a map of this plantation, so I carry it in ma head. I'll get off Master Boadras's land and onto the north road."* Clara touched each of them on the shoulder. *"Once we start running again,"* she warned them, *"don't none of you make*

The Virtual feel

A Slave Girl!

a sound. *If they put the hounds to chasing us, we'll make for the river. If it's those rascals on horseback with their whips, we'll stay to the woods."*

Christina reached out to take Grant's hand. He was trembling like a leaf!

"I want to go home," Grant whispered.

"*Quiet!*" commanded Clara. And they were.

"*Run!*" Clara commanded in a whisper. And they did!

I can't see one foot in front of my face, Christina thought. I can't let her out of my sight or let go of Grant! This is terrible!

It hurt her bare feet to run over the rough dirt clods. She was tired, cold, afraid, and hungry. Things suddenly got worse. Bloodhounds! She could hear them barking and growling close behind them. Run! Christina said to herself. Run faster! They are getting closer! Oh to feel safe again, she thought.

As they rounded the corner and passed an ancient oak tree, dripping with tangled gray beards of Spanish Moss, a hand reached out and grabbed her!

A Slave Girl!

Run. Run!

9 WHERE'S WILL?

All the kids squealed at the same time and ripped off their goggles.

Christina's heart beat so hard it felt like it would burst out of her chest. She took a few slow deep breaths. At first, Christina couldn't see a thing. "Grant, can you see?" she called out. "Is everybody OK? Atty? Duce?"

"I can *now*," Grant answered in a shaky voice.

After carefully removing their gloves, the kids rubbed their eyes for a minute and tried to calm down.

The first joke came from Duce. He said, "Grandpa Will should be happy. It looks like the computer geeks and gurus in Washington finally got these things fixed. Wow!"

The kids finally accepted that they were safe and sound. They were still standing in the same painted footprints on *Freedom Road*. They hadn't moved an inch.

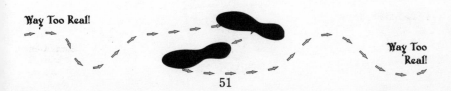

Way Too Real!

Way Too Real!

51

But they *had* been on quite a journey!

Christina looked from face to face. We all have that "deer in the headlights" look, she thought.

Grant asked, "What just happened? Was that real or make believe?"

After a short silence, one at a time, they all began to laugh with relief.

"No it wasn't real, Grant," Christina answered. "It was just pretending. Virtual means like it's real but really not!

"It sure felt real," said Atty. "Just like we were trying to escape on the Underground Railroad. That poor girl!"

"Was she real?" Grant asked. He was still trembling.

"No," Christina said. "Well, the story was a true one. So she was real once. But, well, now *I'm* confused!"

Suddenly Duce said, "Hey! What happened to the William Still journal?" They all glanced at the glass display case, which was completely empty!

"The quilt's gone, too!" said Atty, pointing to the broken glass of that display.

"Grandpa Will! Priscilla!" Atty called. "We've been robbed!"

Way Too Real!

Where's The Journal?

No reply.
Priscilla and Professor Still must be missing, too!

Where Is
Everyone Else?

POOF!

They're
Gone!

10 CRACKED GLASS

They rushed out the door, down the steps, and into the parking lot, calling at the top of their lungs, "Grandpa Will! Priscilla! Professor Still!" Their calls went unanswered.

"It's probably nothing," Atty said. "After all, we *were* a little busy escaping the bloodhounds and slave-catchers. Maybe he told us where he was going, but we just didn't hear him."

"Then how do you explain the empty exhibit case?" demanded Christina.

"Maybe it's a joke," said Duce.

"Not a very funny one," said Grant. "It's a little scary but *not* funny."

"I agree with Grant," Christina said firmly. "It's obvious that the journal and quilt have been stolen and

They're Gone!

POOF!

The Journal
& Quilt Too!

your grandfather and our cousin are missing. The next question is, what do we do about it?"

"Has your grandfather been acting strangely lately, Atty?" Christina asked. "Has he been getting crank phone calls? Or hate mail? Or anything like that?"

Duce replied, "If you mean acting more strangely that he usually does, no! And no mean mail or phone hang-ups, either. Well, at least as far as I know."

Christina continued, "How about financial problems? Does he have any money problems that you know of? Is the journal insured for a lot of money?"

Atty impatiently answered, "*No*, Christina, he doesn't have money problems. And it's his own property, remember? People don't steal from themselves!"

Christina repeated the words over and over that Atty just said to her–his own property–his own property. Christina knew she was missing something here. But what?

"How about enemies?" said Christina, pressing on to her next question. "Has anyone threatened him recently? Has he mentioned being followed when he is in Washington?"

"Christina! Stop this!" Duce said. "Grandpa Will

The Journal &
Quilt Too!

What Do We
Do Now?

is the nicest person I know. He doesn't even kill crickets in his own house. He captures them and takes them back outside."

"Well, can we think of anyone who would like to stop the *Freedom Road* Grand Opening and ruin the July 4th celebration for thousands of people in Philadelphia and the millions of Americans who will be watching it on national TV?" Christina asked.

They were all quiet. Grant sighed, "I don't have even a little clue! And where is Priscilla? Maybe she just went hunting for the professor."

Deep in thought, the kids went back inside the museum. They sat side by side on the floor and stared in silence at the empty exhibit cases.

Something shiny down in the corner, behind the journal exhibit case caught Christina's eye. The shape seemed familiar to her. She crawled over for a closer look. "Well, we have a clue!" she declared.

"Christina, that's not a clue. Those are my grandfather's glasses," said Duce.

"Don't jump to conclusions, Duce," Christina warned. "Do you have any idea why Professor Still wears glasses? Does he need to wear them only for reading?" Christina asked.

What Do
We Do Now?

Professor's
Glasses!

"He wears them because he's as blind as a bat without them," Atty answered.

Christina continued, "Then would it be correct to say that he would never *choose* to go anywhere without his glasses?"

"Absolutely! He always tells us that he can't see two feet in front of his face without them," Atty answered.

"So now we have triple trouble," Christina said firmly. "Priceless historical artifacts have been stolen and Professor Still has been kidnapped. Priscilla, too, probably!"

Peering closely at the glasses, Grant asked, "Did any of you happen to notice that Professor Still's glasses have a big crack down the middle of the right lens? And I think something is stuck to the side ear piece."

Grant paused for breath and then looked shyly over at Duce and added, "Hey, Duce. Be sure Professor Still knows that *I* didn't break his glasses."

"Don't worry, sport, I'll tell him," said Duce.

Christina picked up the glasses and carefully unrolled a slip of yellowed paper, about the size of a fortune cookie message, from the left earpiece. The message was brief and was printed in tiny block letters.

Professor's Glasses!

And A Message!

Christina read it carefully and then told the group, "Listen to this!"

And A Message!

Read This!

11 SHOE CLUE

"What does it say?" the other kids pleaded. Duce tried to snatch the note away, but Christina held tightly to the scrap of paper.

"It says," she began, *"If you want to see him again, follow H.T.'s Friendship Road. You could be a shoe-in."*

Duce said, "Let me see that!" and grabbed the note. Atty, Duce, and Grant gathered around for a better look.

"What does it mean?" asked Grant.

"If we knew the answer, we might know what happened to Grandpa Will," said Duce. "But I have an idea!" He sat down at one of the desktop terminals and signed in to the museum's computer system.

"How did you get Professor Still's password, Duce?" Atty asked suspiciously. "It's supposed to be secret."

"This is no time to worry about details, Atty. This is

What Does
It Mean?

We Need A
Little Help

an emergency. I might have just happened to look over his shoulder one day when he logged on, that's all. It's no big deal, honest!" Duce replied.

Next, Duce went to the museum information search screen and quickly typed in the initials H.T., the + sign, and the words FRIENDSHIP ROAD.

The computer reported that there were 877 matches for the information he had requested. It also told him that 800 of the matches mentioned the same person–Harriet Tubman. While the other three stood behind him to read the screen, Duce clicked on the first choice. A simple picture and brief paragraph appeared.

Harriet Tubman (1821-1913), from Bucktown, Maryland, escaped from slavery and fled to the North when she was about 28 years old. As a conductor on the Underground Railroad, Tubman returned to the South 19 times, risking her life to lead more than 300 slaves to freedom.

"That's got to be it! H.T. must be Harriet Tubman. So we know that much." said Duce.

"Do we all agree that Friendship Road is another name for the Underground Railroad?" Atty asked.

We Need A
Little Help

H.T. is Harriet
Tubman!

Maybe the computer can help!

"I do," Christina said, confidently. "Many people who helped on the Underground Railroad were members of a religious group called the Society of Friends. They were called Quakers, because they believed that they would *quake in their shoes* in God's presence. Quakers were abolitionists. Most of them believed slavery was wrong and should be stopped.

Grabbing her backpack and heading for the door, Christina called over her shoulder, "We'd better get moving because we're 'burning daylight,' as Papa would say. If we start now, maybe we have a chance to save Priscilla and Professor Still."

Looking around for Grant, Christina noticed that her brother was carefully printing something on a big yellow tablet.

"What are you doing, Grant?" she asked.

"I'm leaving a note for Priscilla," Grant answered. "If she comes back, she will be worried about us if we don't leave a note."

"Let me help you with that, Grant," Christina offered. She wrote:

Dear Priscilla:
     We're going to rescue Professor Still

H.T. is Harriet Tubman!

Leaving A Note

and his history. We know you have to stay
with Freedom Road. Be careful. Stay alert.
Keep heading North for the 4th. We'll meet
you by the bell. Don't worry.
Love,
Christina

As the kids stepped out into the late afternoon
sunshine, the *Freedom Road* door closed silently and locked
behind them.

"Which way are we going?" Duce asked.

"North, of course!" Christina answered.

"Do any of you have any ideas about what the shoe
part of the message means? asked Atty.

"I guess we can figure it out as we go," Duce
answered.

Suddenly, Duce took off running for the corner,
waving his arms like a crazy bird. He whistled and yelled,
"Hey! Hey! Pull over!"

A bus approaching the corner slowed to a stop.
Duce hopped on board and spoke to the driver, then turned
and motioned for the rest of the kids to come along. They
ran up to the corner, and hopped on the bus.

Leaving A Note

The Bus
North

After they were seated, Duce explained, "This is the Northside Express. Atty and I have electronic bus passes for the entire Maryland system. The driver let me charge four tickets on my pass. We are now officially heading North!"

"Thanks, Duce," said Christina. "Now all we need is to get a *clue* about a *shoe* so we know what to *do!*"

Her poem brought the groan she expected.

Spying a penny on the bus floor, Christina leaned over to pick it up. *The world looks very different from shoe level,* Christina thought. While looking at the bus floor and everyone's feet, Christina spotted a bright yellow sticky note on Atty's shoe. She gasped.

Atty looked down and peeled the little yellow paper off her shoe and stared at it. "My goodness," she said, "I seem to have the next shoe clue!"

The Bus North

Shoe Clue!

12 SHOE CLUE TWO

"It says," Atty read, "*The feet of the shoemaker's child, Dela, often were bare. Oh what will she ware? Continue if you dare!*"

"Wow," said Christina. "This clue sounds much more ominous. 'Continue if we dare!' This could mean that things are going to get a lot more interesting–and soon."

"Let's not worry about the danger," replied Atty, "until we figure out what the message means."

"We should have at least 30 minutes to solve it," said Duce. "The driver said that his last stop is just beyond the little town of Elkton, Maryland. That's right on the state line.“

"What does a shoemaker have to do with Harriet Tubman and the Underground Railroad?" Christina

Shoe Clue!

To Elkton, Maryland

wondered aloud. She knew that Harriet wasn't a shoemaker. Who was? And where did Harriet's friend the shoemaker live?

"We might be looking for someone who's been dead for more than 100 years," said Christina. "Maybe we can find who we are looking for in the cemetery."

"*In the cemetery?*" groaned Duce. "We don't even know what town we should be going to, and you're sitting there thinking about cemeteries, Christina."

Grant, who had been looking out the window, pointed to an overgrown, kudzu-covered area near the edge of the highway. "If we need a spooky, old cemetery, there's one over there," he said.

Turning to Christina, Grant asked, "Christina, do you remember the time we got locked in that cemetery on Halloween night with Mimi? Or the time Mimi showed us how to make tombstone rubbings in New Orleans?"

Duce and Atty gave each other a resigned look. They figured that they better not argue. They had met Grandmother Mimi several times. They knew that she wrote mysteries for kids and that her kids and grandkids often got into hot water trying to solve them. And somehow they were now smack in the middle of a mystery themselves.

To Elkton, Maryland

Cemetery?

Christina tugged a small, red, spiral notebook and a black marker out of her backpack. She said, "I'll make a list of what we know so far. I'll read it to you as I write. You can tell me if I miss anything." Christina read the five items to the other kids.

1. Harriet Tubman
2. Underground Railroad routes
3. Society of Friends–Quakers
4. Shoemaker has a daughter named Dela.
5. Dela has no shoes to wear.

Atty asked to look at the list. She was keeping both clues safe in a sandwich bag that she had in her pocket. Atty carefully compared Christina's list with the two notes. "The only thing that I notice is that our bad guy can't spell," said Atty.

"What do you mean?" asked Christina.

Pointing to the words on the second clue, Atty explained, "You spelled the word correctly on *your* list, Christina. It should be spelled w-e-a-r. He spelled it incorrectly. He wrote it as w-a-r-e."

Christina wrote it both ways and then looked at the words on the page. "Dela wear and Dela ware," she read.

Cemetery?

Dela Ware?

Looking at her friends with a very smug expression, Christina said, "So all we have to know is which Quaker shoemaker–in Delaware–was an important worker on the Underground Railroad."

"Is *that* all? I know the answer to that one," said Duce.

"Really, what is it?" asked Christina, giving Duce an I-don't believe-you look.

"It's Thomas Garrett! That's got to be right," Duce said.

"Who?" asked Grant. "Do you think Thomas Garrett kidnapped Professor Still?"

"He's not a good choice for the kidnapper, sport." Duce answered, "He's been dead since about 1871. But he's a perfect match! He was a Quaker, a 'stationmaster' on the Underground Railroad, *and* his 'station' was often the attic of the shoe factory he owned in Wilmington, Delaware."

As the bus slowed to a stop, the kids gathered their backpacks and headed to the front. It would be a long walk to Wilmington.

To Wilmington,
Delaware!

A Long Walk
Ahead

Maryland, Delaware and Pennsylvania

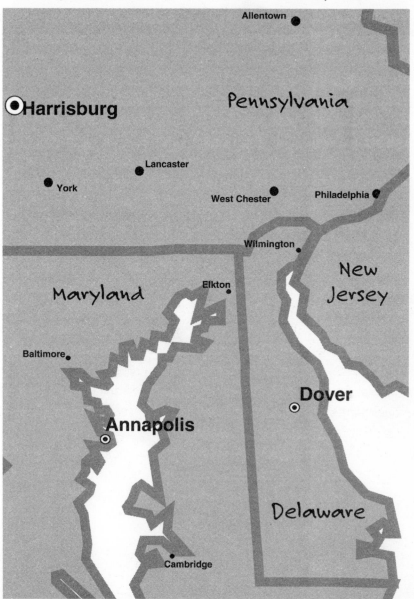

13 HITTING THE WALL

The bus driver had been so nice that Duce stopped to thank him and shake hands before leaving his bus.

"Where are you kids heading? the driver asked. "You're not on the road alone, are you?"

Duce crossed his fingers behind his back and said, "No, sir. But we *are* in sort of a tight spot. We have to be back home in Wilmington by dark, and we are a little low on funds. Do you have any suggestions of how we might safely and cheaply get there before my mother starts to worry about us?"

The kindly driver narrowed his eyes in thought and rubbed his chin. "Well, if you walk up this road about two miles to the Jeffers Diner, and ask to see the manager, I imagine he'd give you a ride back to Wilmington. He gets off work in about an hour, and he lives there. As far as I

A Long Walk
Ahead

To Jeffers
Diner!

know, he goes home when he gets off work."

Amazed, Christina asked, "How do you know that? Why are you being so kind to four people you don't even know?"

"I know it because he's my brother," the driver replied. "My family has been helping travelers in trouble since about 1840." He winked at and left them with these words, "Wherever your travels take you, please stay alert. Stay safe."

That's the third time someone has said that to me today, Christina thought.

Reaching into his pocket for a stub of a pencil and a card, the driver wrote on the back.

> Bud, give nice
> kids a ride to W.
> Call Mom, it's her
> birthday. T.

He gave the card to Christina. With a final wave and toot of the horn, he turned the bus around and headed back to Baltimore.

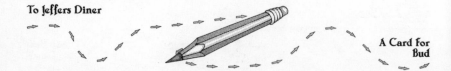

To Jeffers Diner

A Card for Bud

For a minute or two, the kids stood forlornly at the side of road, watching the bus disappear in the distance.

Atty scolded Duce. "It's a very good thing Grandpa Will did not hear you lying to that nice man!"

"Atty, be calm. It was only a little lie, and I was *doing* it *for* Grandpa Will. If he's being held prisoner in Wilmington, we have to save him," Duce replied.

Grant and Christina looked at each other and smiled. She took his hand to keep him safe along the highway.

"Let's get a move on. We're burning daylight," Grant said, sounding just like Papa.

Four tired, foot-sore, hot, thirsty, and dusty kids trudged into the Jeffers Diner. The kids sat at shiny chrome stools and slumped on the counter.

"I feel like a tumbleweed," sighed Christina. "Windblown, dry and dusty."

A kindly voice interrupted her depression. "Why don't you youngsters go in the restroom and wash up, while I make each of you a hot fudge sundae with whipped cream and a tall glass of icy root beer?"

Tiredness was washed away at the restroom sink.

A Card for Bud

To The
Diner

Spirits were restored as the first swallow of icy cold root beer slithered down their parched throats. Grant was soon happily spooning a perfect bite of whipped cream, steamy hot fudge, and sweet rich ice cream into his mouth. He soon wore a hot fudge mustache.

None of the kids had thought about the cost of their sweet treat until the bill was plopped down in front of Christina. Christina peered at the total. Ten dollars! Somehow the ice cream suddenly felt like a rock in her stomach.

A fat, red-faced smiling man in a white apron approached her. "You can ignore that piece of paper, little lady," he said. "Something tells me you were sent here by a special friend of mine," he continued with a smile.

"Are you the manager?" Christina asked.

"Yes, I am," he replied.

Christina suddenly remembered the card in her pocket. Handing it to the big man, Christina said, "Your brother asked us to give this to you. He said you'd be heading home about now and could maybe give us a ride."

"Not a problem," the manager said. "By the time you finish those sundaes, I'll be ready to leave."

Just as Grant noisily sucked the last drops of his root beer, a dark green Dodge mini-van pulled up to the door

At The Counter

How About A Ride?

with the manager at the wheel. The kids piled into the back seats, and they headed toward Wilmington.

The first miles passed in absolute silence. Each person was busy with their thoughts. Keeping his eyes safely on the road, the manager looked at the reflections of Grant and Christina in his rear-view mirror.

"Where exactly do you need to be dropped off?" he asked. "I can plan my route accordingly."

Wanting to tell the truth, Christina replied, "I'm not sure of the exact address but we'd like to be dropped off at the shoe factory that was owned by Thomas Garrett." Christina added, "He was a station master on the Underground Railroad, you know."

The manager looked at her longer this time, his eyes narrowing as he thought about her request. Then he replied, "I've lived in Wilmington my entire life, but I don't know where his shoe factory was. I can take you to the Historical Society and you can ask them. And I'm *pretty* sure this is one of the days that the Thomas Garrett home is open to the public. Would one of those two places do?"

Oh, no, Christina thought. The clue talked about shoes *not* houses or historical societies. I have to choose something, but they could *both* be wrong!

Noticing her hesitation, he asked, "What exactly are

How About
A Ride?

No More
factory?

you looking for? Are you interested in the Underground Railroad? Maybe I can help because I happen to know a lot about the Underground Railroad. The National Park Service has identified 380 Underground Railroad sites nationwide. I'm proud to say that 19 of them are right here in Delaware."

"My family is even planning a trip to Cincinnati to see the new Underground Railroad museum, the National Underground Railroad Freedom Center. I hear it's a doozy. This Freedom Center plans to set up 60 Freedom Stations throughout the country to give researchers and teachers an easy way to learn the stories and use the lessons of the Underground Railroad."

Christina came straight to the point. "We're looking for Professor William Still on a matter of great urgency. We have reason to believe that we'll find him at Thomas Garrett's old shoe factory. If there isn't a factory, I'm afraid that I may have gotten the clue–uh–I mean the message wrong."

Atty tried to cover Christina's slip up. She said, "I'm very interested in the Underground Railroad. It's nice to meet an expert. Could you tell us a few of your favorite Wilmington escape stories, sir? Where did the slaves hide? How did slaves move from station to station?"

No More
Factory?

Looking For
The Professor

Temporarily distracted from his earlier question, the manager eagerly responded. "They had to hide in the daytime. It was only safe to operate *this* railroad at night. Lots of folks who hid slaves lived in one-room houses. These farmers hid the escaping slaves under the house floor in the root cellar, where vegetables were stored. The root cellar was usually small, dirty, and dark. All kinds of critters shared that hiding place!"

"How about snakes? Did they have snakes?" Grant asked.

"Yes, I'm sure they sometimes had a snake slither in for a visit," the manager answered.

"I can't imagine staying quiet if a bug was crawling up my neck," said Christina.

"Bet I could do it," bragged Grant.

"You were right about old Thomas Garrett hiding slaves in his shoe factory," the manager went on. "He hid them behind a false wall of shoe shelves in his warehouse. It looked solid, but Garrett had it specially built so he could pull the wall out and hide slaves in the room behind it. I think a piece of that shoe wall might be on display at the Garrett home. It's been turned into a museum, you know."

He continued, "I heard that on one of Harriet Tubman's trips, she arrived before dawn at Garrett's

Looking for
The Professor

S-s-s-s!
Snakes

factory with nine escaped slaves. Well now, Garrett didn't have any more room at the factory. So, he gave each slave a new pair of shoes and gave Harriet some money. Then he had them lay down–side by side–in his delivery wagon. He'd put a false floor in the wagon that could be pulled out just like the false wall in his factory. He put all 10 of those people in the wagon bottom and then drove them right by the slave catchers!

"Station masters *and* conductors had to be brave, smart, and quick-thinking," he said. "Another time, Garrett hid slaves in caskets and took them out of town in hearses as part of a real funeral procession!" he concluded.

Christina had heard what she was listening for. If the shoe wall was at the Garrett home, she bet that's where they'd find Professor Still.

"If you let us out on the corner closest to the Thomas Garrett house, that would be perfect," she told the manager.

A few minutes later, the green van pulled up right in front the Garrett house.

"There you go, kids. Curbside service," the manager said. "Good luck finding Professor Still."

The kids dashed up front steps just as the volunteer was closing the house for the day.

S-s-s-s!
Snakes

Curbside
Service

"Did you see a distinguished-looking, balding, black gentleman in a shirt like ours visiting earlier in the day?" asked Duce.

"No," the volunteer answered, as she tried to shoo the kids out the door.

Quickly, Duce explained that they had come all the way from Baltimore just to see the shoe case wall. "Would you please give us just a minute to see it," he pleaded.

She pointed up the stairs. "It's the entire wall of the bedroom on the right," she said in an aggravated voice. "Please hurry."

The kids bounded up the stairs and into the room. Instantly, they started tapping on the wall panels calling "Professor Still! Grandpa Will! Can you hear us? Are you in there?"

There was only silence. Christina groaned. Were they too late to rescue Professor Still? Had they missed him at this Underground Railroad station? It's not looking good, Christina thought, but we're not giving up!

Curbside
Service

Please Hurry!

14 THE WILMINGTON STATION

Undaunted, Grant continued to press the panels behind the lowest shelves while the taller kids tackled the upper levels. "I found something," Grant said.

He turned around holding a small white envelope with a single word written on it. The word was STILL.

The other kids tried to snatch it out of his hand, but Grant wasn't letting that happen. "Don't touch it. It's mine!" he yelled.

"Ok, it's yours," agreed Christina. "Please open it, Grant, and let us read it."

Grant carefully opened the envelope and pulled out a card. He looked at it for a few seconds and handed it over to Duce. "Here Duce, you can read it for me."

Duce read: *"You're too late. So, I have him–still. Flying gourds make a clatter. Use them to get to the root of the*

Please Hurry!

Still

Can Gourds fly?

matter."

Duce's shoulders slumped. He let the note flutter to the floor. Then he walked to the top of the stairs and slowly sat down. He held his head in his hands and didn't say anything for a few minutes. Atty grabbed the note and stuffed it in her baggie of clues.

The volunteer came to the bottom of the stairs and saw Duce. "Are you feeling alright?" she asked.

Duce shook off his disappointment as he rose to his feet. "Yes," he replied. "Thank you for asking. We'll be heading out now, so you can close the museum."

As they walked up the block, Christina said, "We're following the route of escaping slaves and chasing an escaping kidnapper, our next step is obvious."

"Obvious?" said Atty. "It's not very obvious to me!"

"We've got to walk North until we find a gourd tree," Christina told them.

"It's better than just standing here, Christina," said Atty, "but I have two problems with it."

"What?" asked Christina.

"Gourds don't grow on trees. They grow on vines. And how do we find North in the daytime? Don't we need to use the North Star as our compass?" asked Atty.

Grant had the solution. "If we need help, we can use

Can Gourds
Fly?

Compass In
The Sky

my whistle," he said.

Christina said, "That just doesn't make any sense."

"Sure it does," Grant replied.

He pulled his red whistle from under his shirt.

"Mimi gave it to me," Grant explained. He put the whistle to his lips and blew. It shrilled, TWEEEEEET!

"Point us in the right direction, sport," said Duce.

Grant spun around and pointed his finger in a lucky guess, and they began walking.

A little over an hour later, Grant came to a full stop and sat down. "I need to rest," he said. "I think I've walked my feet down to stumps."

They looked around in search of a place to rest. Nearby stood a horse farm's white, wooden fence. A beautiful old, white oak tree grew beside the fence. Christina remembered Mimi telling her that in olden times, farmers who plowed their fields with horses called these giant shade trees, "Resting Trees." They were left in the field on purpose to provide shelter from the sun for the farmer and his horses.

Pointing toward it, Christina said, "Let's rest there." She told them the story of the Resting Tree as they walked

Compass In
The Sky

Resting
Tree

across the field.

As the kids got closer to the tree, they heard an odd noise. It reminded Grant of the *clanking, clunking* noise that his Mom's pottery wind chimes made when a breeze blew across their back porch.

Christina raced ahead. When she got to the tree, she looked up and motioned for the others to hurry over. She was staring up into the branches.

Hanging from the tree branches were dozens of drinking gourds. They *clunked* and *clanked* in the wind.

"I think we've found our drinking gourd tree!" said Christina.

"What do they drink?" Grant asked. "I don't see a mouth?"

"They don't drink, Grant," said Christina. "Slaves drank water *from* them. Instead of a fancy metal dipper, slaves used a hollowed-out gourd to scoop water out of a bucket. A gourd is a kind of squash."

"So how do we get to the 'root of the matter'?" asked Atty.

"I don't know that yet," Christina replied.

The kids sat with their backs to the giant tree. Bored, Grant pulled two small plastic soldiers from his pocket. He used the roots of the tree for a battlefield.

Resting
Tree

Root Of The
Matter

Is that a Resting Tree?

Something shiny in the earth caught his eye.

Using his soldier like a spoon, Grant dug furiously. He soon uncovered something that looked like very old. He held the object in his dirty little hands, turning it left and right.

"I think it's a magic lamp," Grant said. "I found it so I get to make three wishes! I will wish for a hot fudge sundae, some cookies, and a giant pizza. Hmmm. Do you think that that would be one wish or three?" he asked.

Duce looked at Grant's treasure. "I saw something like this in the *Freedom Road*. I think it's an oil lamp. Pioneers filled it with whale oil. A wick goes in that spout thing. They'd burn for hours and were easier and safer to carry than a candle."

Grant didn't like that explanation, so he ignored it. He rubbed the lamp and called out, "Genie, come forth!" Nothing happened. So he tossed the lamp down and went back to playing with his toy soldiers.

Christina picked up the lamp and tugged on its top. Off it popped. She put two fingers inside and felt around.

"Empty," she said, "not a drop of whale oil left." Then her fingers touched what felt like a piece of paper that was rolled up tightly and placed in the spout like a wick. "Well, maybe not *completely* empty," she said.

Root Of The
Matter

Genie, Come
forth!

She pulled out the paper and unrolled it.

Duce grabbed it from her hand. "My turn!" he said.

"Now that you've taken it, you could at least be polite enough to read it," Christina told him. It was almost too dark to see the writing. Duce squinted at it.

He began, *"Time is short. No time for play. In the place that replays the Underground Railway."*

Christina was still thinking about the clue as her eyes started to droop. She was sound asleep in seconds, beneath the spooky Resting Tree.

Genie, Come forth!

Another Clue

15 THE LAST BREATH

By the time the sun rose over the meadow, the kids were bumping along the road in the back of a farmer's vegetable truck headed for Lancaster, Pennsylvania.

"So how did you figure it out, Atty?" Christina asked.

"It came to me while I was asleep," Atty answered. "When I was about Grant's age, my parents took us to Lancaster to see the Underground Railroad re-enactment at the AME church in Lancaster."

"What's a reenactment?" Grant asked. "And what's AME stand for?"

"AME stands for African Methodist Episcopal. A reenactment is like a play," Atty answered. "Only the actors perform in an open setting instead of playing their parts and saying their lines on a stage. Reenactments are

Another Clue

To Lancaster!

based on historical happenings instead of make-believe."

Atty continued, "We took a bicycle tour and visited several Underground Railroad stations in the area. Our favorite stop was the station that had a reenactment *and* lunch."

"Breakfast *or* lunch sounds really good to me right now," said Grant. "Did we bring my wishing lamp?" he asked Christina. "Maybe we can trade it at the farmers' market for some sausage and biscuits." Grant's wishing lamp was tucked safely into Christina's bulging backpack.

The farmer treated the kids to breakfast and dropped them off just a few blocks from the *Living The Reenactment Site*. He assured them that they were indeed headed due north.

"Told ya!" said Grant. The other kids just shook their heads.

Christina was first in line when the ticket booth opened. The lady smiled at her and asked, "What name is your reservation under?"

"It should be under Still," Christina guessed. The lady flipped though the ticket envelopes and pulled out an envelope that said Still.

"I have four tickets for *Still*," the reservations lady said and handed Christina the envelope."

To
Lancaster!

We Have
Tickets!

"How'd you know we had tickets?" Grant asked.

"I just had a feeling we'd have them," Christina answered. "I hope we have *more* than just tickets inside."

"The shuttle for the reenactment at the church leaves in five minutes," the lady told the kids. "Or you might want to use your ticket at the station and sample a traditional 1800s Pennsylvania Dutch farm meal."

Christina opened the envelope and removed its contents. It held four light blue tickets and one light blue piece of paper. On the paper was the small block lettering that was becoming all too frighteningly familiar to the kids.

Hidden in
plain sight.

"Last night's message told us that 'time is running out' and that we have 'no time to play'," said Christina. "I think that means that we don't have time to go to the reenactment *play*."

"Agreed." said Duce. "We should go to the farm house, have the meal, and 'look for the obvious'."

The farm hosts served scrapple and applesauce. Then they showed the visitors how to use ground corn meal to make soupy yellow batter. They poured it into flat, cast-iron skillets and cooked it over an open fire to create Johnnycakes.

Christina mixed her batter but decided that there was *no way in the entire world she would ever eat one bite of it*. The corn meal had bugs in it! Duce told her not to worry and suggested that she think about the weevils as a protein source. How gross!

When the time came to take their skillets out of the fire, Christina put hers on a small metal square that she *thought* was a hot plate. It was actually a pressure plate—like a button.

The weight of the iron skillet on the pressure plate caused a trap door in the earthen floor of the old kitchen to magically slide open. There in the root cellar was Professor Still! They'd found him!

"Is he alive?" Grant asked, peering down into the hole.

To The Station

Professor Still!

No time to play!

"Of course he's alive, Grant," said Christina. "The question should be–is he alright?"

Duce rushed past them and bolted down the rickety stairs.

Professor Still was blindfolded and tied to an old wooden armchair. His blindfold was a scuba diver's mask that had its face plate painted black. Sitting next to his chair was a bright green scuba air tank. The scuba breathing device was taped to Professor Still's mouth. A sheet of yellow notebook paper was pinned to his shirt.

Duce removed the mask. Grant and Atty went to work untying the ropes. Christina got a warm wet cloth and carefully peeled the tape off Professor Still's face.

Once he was freed from his restraints, they brought him a glass of water and rubbed his arms and legs to bring back his circulation.

Sitting at Professor Still's side, rubbing his hand, Christina glanced down at the air tank. She felt her face go pale and she felt a little faint. The air **gauge** showed that one minute of air was all that remained in the tank!

When Professor Still felt strong enough, they helped him stand and climb out of his tiny prison.

He was battered and bruised, but his sense of humor was totally undamaged. "I'd say, good to see you,"

Professor Still!

Thank Goodness!

he told them, "but I've lost my glasses and can't see two inches in front of my face." He continued, "Did any of you adventurers find my eye glasses in your travels?"

"Duce has them, Professor Still," said Grant. "And Duce wants to tell you that I didn't break them."

"I'm sure you didn't, young Grant," replied Professor Still, settling his battered, wire-rimmed glasses back in place on his face. Professor Still regarded them kindly for a very long minute. Each child basked in his silent approval and appreciation.

How does he do that? Christina wondered. He can hug us with a glance. I know he's proud of us and he didn't say a word about it. I wonder if I can learn to do that?

"How did you get down there?!" asked one of the adults in the crowd that had gathered around.

"I was kidnapped," the professor said, and everyone gasped.

"How did you survive?" another adult asked.

The professor chuckled. "My father named me William *B. Still* for a purpose, I suppose!"

"But where is Priscilla?" asked Christina. "Wasn't she kidnapped too?"

Professor Still just looked puzzled. For the first

Thank
Goodness!

A Job for
The Kids

time, the professor noticed the kids' dirty, stained, rumpled appearance. "Let's get all of you cleaned up and back on the road," Professor Still told them. "I have an important job for you to do."

"What job?" asked Christina.

"I need you to get the William Still Journal and the Harriet Tubman quilt back to the *Freedom Road* before the Grand Opening. They are still missing, and I'm counting on *you* to rescue them!"

A Job for
The Kids

Find The
Journal &
Quilt

16 BIG MAN IN TOWN

In less than 30 minutes, the kids were showered, combed, in clean clothes, and ready to leave. The local people had been more than happy to help them. Christina could sense the spirit of helplessness that had been part of the Underground Railroad experience for so many slaves.

"Professor Still, why aren't you coming with us?" asked Grant.

"I need to get back to the *Freedom Road*. Priscilla and I have a lot of work to do. While you were showering, I contacted Priscilla to let her know that we're all safe and back on the job."

"Thank goodness she's safe!" said Christina. "We were afraid that she was kidnapped too."

"No," Professor Still assured her. "She had just gone to town for supplies. She was so worried when she

Where Is
Priscilla?

Priscilla Is
Safe!

103

returned and found all of us *vanished!*" he said with a wide sweep of his bony, black arm.

"Are we heading out again without a lead?" asked Christina.

"Oh we have something to go on," said Professor Still. "We now know something more about this thief and kidnapper."

"What's that?" asked Christina.

"He wants to be famous," Professor Still told her. "He seems to see what he's doing as a way to be right smack in the middle of the national media spotlight. I'll read you the message that he left pinned to my shirt."

Professor Still read: *Still took the fame but everyone will soon know my name.*

"That makes sense," said Christina. "He's going to Philadelphia because that's where the TV cameras will be."

"What if we don't find the journal and quilt before the grand opening? Will you have to cancel it?" asked Christina.

"We won't cancel it. We've given our word and we won't go back on it, Christina," said Professor Still.

"Having the grand opening without the most important two items in the exhibit *would* be like trying to have Thanksgiving Dinner without the turkey," said Atty.

Priscilla Is Safe!

Why Steal Them?

"It's still great to get together, but something very important would be missing," Duce agreed.

"Now let's get you on your way," said Professor Still. "These nice people tell me that someone going to Philadelphia has offered to give you a ride."

A dark green sedan immediately pulled up in front of the reenactment building and tooted its horn.

"Now that's what I call service," said Christina.

Professor Still leaned forward and stuck his head in the car's window. Looking at the driver, Professor Still asked, "Do I know you?"

The driver shook his head 'no.' He quickly wrote a single word on a note pad and held it up to the window. It said *Laryngitis.*"

The professor nodded and handed some money to the driver for gas and said, "I want you to take these fine people to Philadelphia. They'll tell you where they want to go when you arrive." The driver nodded.

The kids got in and the car roared onto the highway, squealing its tires.

"That's not very safe driving," said Christina

"Doesn't this car have seatbelts?" asked Grant, scrounging around in the back seat to find them.

"I'll tell you something that it *does* have," Duce

Why Steal Them?

Off To Philly!

observed.

"What?" asked Atty.

"Paper stuck down in the seat. I can't get it out–my fingers must be too big," said Duce.

"Let me try," said Christina. "Look! It's a clue!"

Christina quietly read it to the other kids. It says, "*Big Man In Town.*"

Atty asked, "Does anybody know if the president or any other famous people are visiting Philadelphia?"

Christina took her Underground Railroad guidebook out of her backpack and turned to the section for Philadelphia. "Lots of important and influential people have come from Philadelphia," Christina told them.

After flipping through pages of her guidebook for a few minutes, Christina said, "I think William Penn might be the Big Man In Town. Listen to this:

> *Atop City Hall stands a statue of William Penn.*
>
> *It is 37 feet tall. It is the biggest statue on top of*
>
> *a United States building.*"

Christina raised her voice and said, "Mr. Driver, please take us to the Philadelphia City Hall."

Off To Philly!

Big Man in Town

The kids eventually found themselves on the observation deck on top of City Hall and at the base of the giant statue. They walked around the observation deck searching for their next clue. Philadelphia traffic whizzed around the base of the building at frantic speeds.

"It looks like a toy town from up here," Grant said. Looking from left to right and seeing nothing new to interest him, Grant asked, "Has anyone found a clue?"

Just for fun, he raised his face and arm into the air and called, "We're waiting for a clue!"

Statues, tall buildings, and pigeons just seem to go together. No sooner had Grant asked his question than a passing pigeon dropped a large spat of pigeon poop right into his hair! Grant didn't know if he wanted to laugh or cry. Pigeon poop was so funny when he said it out loud that he decided to laugh. "I've been pigeon pooped!" he said and giggled.

"Next time remember to duck, sport," suggested Duce.

"Uh oh! Incoming pigeon!" Grant warned.

This pigeon didn't poop and run. She gently glided to a stop on the railing and walked along to Christina's

Big Man In Town

Pigeon Poop!

outstretched hand.

"Maybe she is a secret agent pigeon, sent by the Big Man," Christina wondered.

"Could be," Atty said. "Look at her leg. See that band? I think she is a specially trained messenger pigeon. If that's true, Christina, I think she'll step onto your hand and let you remove the message she's brought."

Christina carefully cradled the pigeon close to her chest and pulled the message roll out of its holder. Then she gently placed the pigeon back on the railing.

"Sorry, girl," said Christina. "I don't have a return message for you. But thanks for dropping by."

The bird flew off.

Christina carefully unrolled the narrow paper and read the message.

"What does it say?" asked Grant. "Do we know what to do next?"

"I think so," answered Christina.

The message was passed around. It said:

Pigeon Poop!

Pigeon With
A Message

You crack
me up. Let
freedom ring.

"That clue cracks *me* up!" said Grant, still scrubbing at his hair.

"Sounds like our next stop is the Liberty Bell!" said Christina. "We can take the trolley over to Old Town and get off at Independence Square. If we can figure out where he's hidden the journal and quilt, we can get them back for Professor Still."

"When we get them back, he'll be outsmarted. He will *stay* a loser in the fame game," said Duce.

"*If* we get them back," Atty said, with a hopeless shrug. "This seems like a wild goose chase to me."

The kids boarded a bright red trolley at the corner that was heading into the area known as the Historic Mile.

"Some of the most famous historical sites in America lie along this route. The problem for us is that there are more hiding places than we can even imagine,"

Pigeon With
A Message

To The
Liberty Bell!

said Christina.

"For example," she continued, referring to her guidebook, "the Betsy Ross house would be a great place to hide a quilt. Since Betsy was a seamstress, lots of fabric would probably be laying around."

"If the journal is hidden in Library Hall, it would take us years to find it because all the books in there are really old," said Duce.

"Why are all the books old?" asked Grant.

"Library Hall was the first library opened to the public in America. It was started in 1731 by Ben Franklin and some of his friends," explained Duce.

"They must have really liked to read," said Grant.

Christina sighed, "There must be thousands of hiding places in Independence Hall too."

"Hello, folks," said the voice of the trolley tour guide over the speakers. *"On our way to the Historic Mile today, I'm going to tell you about some of the fabulous food that's helped put Pennsylvania on the map. Does anyone here like bubble gum?"*

Grant quickly called out, "I do!"

The other passengers laughed.

"We have one bubble gum fan in the house," said the guide. *"Here's a fact for you to chew on. Bubble Gum was*

To The
Liberty Bell!

fabulous
Philly food

created by accident in 1928 by Walter E Diemer."

"*Our second most famous Philadelphia food mistake was the invention of the ice cream soda. A drug store soda jerk accidentally dropped a scoop of ice cream into a glass of soda. The customer loved it! Anyone here like chocolate?"*

Chocolate got a round of applause from the passengers.

"*Well, Pennsylvania is the home of Hershey Foods, where they make all those delicious Hershey kisses. On the average day, 33 million kisses come off their assembly lines. It takes about 50,000 cows to produce the milk used for just one day's worth of Hershey's milk chocolate!"*

"*By the way,"* the guide said, "*Root beer was first made in Philadelphia in 1877."*

The guide concluded, "*Our next trolley stop is the home of Betsy Ross. She sewed the first U.S. flag! If that is your destination, please gather your belongings and wait until the trolley has come to a complete stop."*

The Betsy Ross House hadn't been where the kids planned to stop next until Christina leaped off the trolley as it slowed at a corner. With no idea of where she was headed or where they were going, the other kids dashed after her. They shouted for her to stop. And she did–about a block later. She took a few steps to the left and to the

Fabulous
Philly Food

Off The
Trolley

right searching the sidewalk in both directions.

"Where did that guy go?" Christina demanded. "Did you see which direction he went?"

"I've no idea, Christina," said Duce. "Who in the world are you talking about? Who were *you* chasing? I only know that we were chasing *you.*"

"*I* was chasing Ichabod Crane," she told them. "And I lost him."

Off The Trolley

Chasing Crane?

17 RING RING

"I don't mean the character Ichabod Crane from the creepy *Legend of Sleepy Hollow,*" Christina explained. "I mean an Ichabod Crane-*looking* person."

Turning to Atty, Christina asked, "How would you describe Ichabod Crane?"

"Tall, very thin with legs that are too long in trousers that are too short," Atty began. "Large nose and elephant ears, scrawny neck–the kind my grandfather would call a turkey neck–and that funny deep knee bending kind of walk."

"Exactly," agreed Christina. "As we were riding along in the trolley, I realized that I had seen *the same man* in *three different towns*!"

"Mimi says that there are no such things as coincidence in mysteries," Grant reminded her.

Chasing Crane?

Coincidence?

"Why didn't you tell us about him before, Christina?" asked Atty.

"I didn't even think about it until I saw him again a few minutes ago, and then it clicked," Christina explained. "I first saw him at the restaurant in Baltimore. The driver who brought us to Philadelphia had the same profile. When I saw the same guy here, I just *had* to follow him."

"He could just be a tourist who's interested in the Underground Railroad. Nothing mysterious in that," Duce told her.

Christina knew that but just seeing Ichabod made the hair on the back of her neck stand up. Shaking off the eerie feeling, she was ready to move on to the next stop. She knew that they could easily walk to the Liberty Bell in just a few minutes. That was certainly the place where history got cracked up.

The line outside the Liberty Bell was long. So, Duce waited in line while Grant, Christina and Atty went to a street vendor and came back with giant, brown, salty soft pretzels and root beers–two more of Pennsylvania's famous foods. Pretzels were invented in Lancaster–where they rescued Professor Still. Root beer was first made in Philadelphia in 1866. Sometimes, Christina thought, history could be delicious.

Coincidence?

To The
Liberty Bell!

Standing back in line, looking at the Liberty Bell, Christina tried to imagine how scared, tired, and hopeful slaves on the Underground Railroad must have been. "Let freedom ring!" she said aloud.

They were finally admitted into the Liberty Bell **Pavilion**. Christina worked her way through the crowd to get close to the park ranger who was telling the story of the Liberty Bell's history. Christina also hoped to get a peek inside the enormous bell.

The park ranger welcomed the group and asked where they were all from. People in their group had come from all across America and around the world.

The ranger explained, "The Liberty Bell was cast–made in England in 1752. So much has been written and told about the bell that it is now very hard to tell the difference between fact and fiction. Anti-slavery groups in Philadelphia were said to be inspired by the bell's inscription: *Proclaim liberty throughout all the land unto all the inhabitants thereof.*

The ranger continued, "After traveling all the way from England, the first time the bell was rung, it cracked! No one could repair it, so a new one was ordered."

"The second bell hung in that building that we see behind us. It was rung on July 8, 1776, to call all the

To The
Liberty Bell!

Let freedom
Ring!

citizens together. Since people didn't have radio or television in those days, when there was big news to tell bells were rung to call the people to the town square. The big news on that July day was to tell everyone that a new country had been formed a few days earlier on July 4. Its name: The United States of America!"

The Ranger concluded, "Later that afternoon, in the assembly room of Independence Hall, delegates gathered to sign the Declaration of Independence. This bell was on display in that location until 1976 when this Pavilion was built for the U.S Bicentennial."

Christina and the kids approached the ranger. "What's inside the Liberty Bell?" she asked him."

"Well, it had better be empty," he told the kids.

"Are you *absolutely* sure?" Christina asked. "I noticed that it's more than two feet off the ground. I could imagine a little boy–about my brother's size–sneaking under the velvet rope and leaving a wad of bubble gum inside."

"Oh you can, can you?" said the ranger. He turned and glared at Grant. "Did you put gum in the Liberty Bell, young man?"

"No, sir, I would never do that," Grant answered. "But that doesn't mean that some other little kid didn't do

Let Freedom
Ring!

What's Inside
The Bell?

it." Quickly, Grant added, "I'm just the right size to check on that for you."

Without waiting for a reply, Grant slipped under the rope *and* under the lip of the bell.

"Hey, kid! Come back here now!" the ranger yelled.

Grant acted like he was stuck under the bell. He stumbled back and forth with a soft *BONG BONG* against its sides.

Before the ranger could grab him, Grant popped out from beneath the bell and ran past him. "No gum!" he shouted.

What's Inside The Bell?

No Gum!

18 STICK 'EM UP

Grant's shirt bulged with what he found inside the bell. He wasn't a bit frightened by the other kids' threatening looks. He was now the center of attention and he was loving it.

"Come on, Grant," Duce urged. "Let us read it. This isn't about us, it's about America. Millions of people will be watching the July 4th celebration from right here in Independence Square tomorrow. The *Freedom Road* will pull up right here next to the Liberty Bell Pavilion. It's the perfect chance to help people learn about the importance of freedom and helping others. That was what the Underground Railroad was all about."

Atty said, "Mimi and Papa will be so disappointed if we don't recover the quilt and journal in time. We have to do all that we can do, Grant, to protect freedom. This is

No Gum!

Protect freedom!

119

your part."

Grant's small chin quivered and his big blue eyes filled with tears. "Well, gee," he said, "I was just playing around. And you guys got serious all of a sudden. Can't you take a joke?"

Reaching under his shirt, Grant removed a fat envelope from the waistband of his pants and handed it to Christina. She tore the envelope open and pulled out an oversized post card.

"Read it!" the kids demanded.

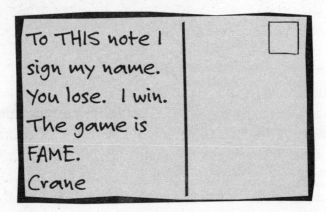

To THIS note I
sign my name.
You lose. I win.
The game is
FAME.
Crane

"'Sign his name?'" Christina wondered aloud. "We have to get to the Assembly Hall before it's too late."

Turning to Grant, Christina looked into his eyes. "Grant," she said, "we're all depending on you. If you see

Protect
freedom!

Quick! To
Assembly Hall!

A clue to decipher!

trouble heading our way while we're searching the Assembly Hall, blow your whistle three times. I'm afraid this Crane character might destroy the journal and quilt on national television–just to get his 15 minutes of fame!"

Christina, Atty, and Duce ran across the commons and through the side door of Independence Hall at top speed. Stopping at the door of the Assembly Hall, Christina paused to imagine the Declaration of Independence being *signed* in this room. Then Christina had one of her hunches. Crane's clue had stressed that he was *signing* his name. The journal and quilt must be hidden in the room where the Declaration of Independence was *signed*!

Turning to Duce and Atty, Christina said, "I think we have about 10 minutes before a park ranger comes in here with the next tour group. Let's look under all the furniture, starting with the main table where the Declaration of Independence was signed."

In the back corner under the table top they discovered two packages duct–taped in place. Christina gently pulled the tape away from the smaller package first.

It was wrapped in cloth. As she peeled back the edge, she could see the corner of the brown leather journal. They'd found it!

Quick! To
Assembly Hall!

found Them!

Next, they eased the quilt out from under the table. As they carefully peeled the tape away from the quilt package, they heard an urgent warning: TWEET! TWEET! TWEET!

"I'll take my packages back, right now!" commanded a voice from the doorway. Someone stepped from the dim hallway into the sunlit Assembly Room, and Christina recognized the man she'd been calling Ichabod, disguised as a Park Ranger.

"Don't make me hurt you. Just slide both packages over here, and I won't have to use this," he growled.

Crane had something in his hand. Was it a gun? Christina froze for a moment. Atty moved into action. Putting all of her soccer skills to work, she dropkicked Christina's backpack into the center of Crane's chest.

"Oooooffff!" With the wind knocked out of him, Crane fell over with a thud.

The kids pounced on him in a second. Duce plunked down on his chest. Atty and Christina grabbed his wrists. When the man squirmed and squealed, Grant slapped both his hands over the man's mouth. "Hush up, Itch-a-bod!" Grant ordered.

A CNN reporter, who had been setting up for the celebration, rushed in through the courtyard doors with his

Found Them!

Oh No!

cameraman jogging behind him. He called, "Cut! Great! We got the whole thing! The lead for tonight's national news will be Kids Foil Madman's Attempt to Steal National Treasures!

Next, the front door burst open. They were immediately surrounded by park rangers, Mimi and Papa, and several other VIPs.

"What's going on here?" one of the rangers demanded of the kids. "Why are you assaulting this ranger?"

"He's not a real park ranger," said Christina. "He's an imposter and a criminal!"

"These young people are on special assignment from the *Freedom Road* Underground Railroad Exhibit and they are American heroes!" exclaimed Mimi.

Grant rushed up and threw his arms around Mimi.

"Mimi, Mimi! You came!"

Giving him a big hug, Mimi said, "Of course, I did Grant. You whistled, didn't you?"

What's Going
On Here?

You
Whistled?

19 FAME AND CRANE

The *Freedom Road* rolled up in front of Liberty Bell Pavilion as a Philadelphia policeman and an agent from the FBI walked out with their prisoner, Benjamin Crane.

It took Professor Still and Priscilla a long time to explain. Benjamin Crane had taken Professor Still's freshman history class the same year as Priscilla. He won a national history research competition and a full scholarship. Crane was scheduled to be interviewed on *Sixty Minutes* and *Good Morning America* television shows.

Then Professor Still had discovered that the research was actually stolen from another student. Crane was expelled from school and no one had heard from him since. However, he had obviously remained bitter and felt that the world owed him something–whether or not he

cheated.

"It seems," Priscilla explained, "Crane was working as a waiter at the City Lights restaurant in Baltimore when Professor Still told us the story of the Still Journal and the Tubman Quilt. Crane originally planned to steal both things and then pretend to find the valuable journal and quilt minutes before the ribbon cutting."

"I guess he imagined that would make him a national hero and give him the fame he thought had been stolen from him 10 years earlier, when I caught him cheating," concluded Professor Still.

Crane admitted to the police that he had planted the clues in hopes of keeping the "troublesome" kids out of his hair.

"You don't have a brain, Ichabod," Grant said, "'cause we figures out your clues!" The kids laughed until Mimi gave them a BIG frown.

"This man is in serious trouble," Mimi said sternly.

It seemed to take forever for Christina and the rest of the kids to explain about following the Underground Railroad, gourd trees, virtual reality goggles, magic lamps, johnnycakes, quilt codes, and Christina's hunch about

Explaining
Crane

Explaining
Themselves

Ichabod Crane. The kids got tired of explaining, and the adults got tired of not understanding and so the matter was finally got dropped when Mimi's cell phone rang.

Mimi said, "Hello." After listening carefully to the person on the other end, Mimi said, "Yes, I'll hold for the President of the United States!"

Mimi held her finger to her lips to keep them quiet for a moment while she listened. This is how it sounded on her end of the conversation. "Yes. Yes. I'll tell them. Thank you. Good-bye, Mr. President. You, too, sir."

"Tell! Tell!" the kids squealed, after she hung up.

"The President was just calling to thank you kids for helping protect America's history by rescuing three of our important national treasures," Mimi relayed.

"*Three* treasures, Mimi?" Christina asked, counting in her head. "The quilt. The journal. What's the third national treasure?"

"The third treasure is a *who* not a *what*. The third treasure is Professor Still," Mimi told them. The professor smiled humbly.

"Mimi, I need to ask you just one more thing," said Grant.

"What's that?" Mimi answered.

"If I blow my whistle again, do you think you could

Explaining
Themselves

Three
Treasures!

come running with something special to eat?"

"What special food do you want, Grant?" Mimi asked.

"He wants cake, Mimi," said Christina.

"I think we can handle that. Any other requests?" Mimi asked.

"Just one," pleaded Grant. "It has to be *real* cake this time. I don't want crab cakes or johnnycakes. I just want chocolate cake . . .with French fries on the side."

"Grant," boomed Papa. "*You* take the cake!"

"Hey!" said Priscilla, with a snap of her fingers. "I know a great bakery nearby. It's underground."

"We could take the railroad to get there," Papa and Mimi suggested.

"No *underground*," begged Christina.

"No *railroad*," insisted Grant.

"*Just cake*!" said Grant.

"It's the Fourth of July," Priscilla reminded them. "Will *birthday* cake do?"

"As long as it's CAKE!" said Grant, and everyone laughed.

The End

Do we have to explain any more?

ABOUT THE AUTHOR

   Carole Marsh is an author and publisher who has written many works of fiction and non-fiction for young readers. She travels throughout the United States and around the world to research her books. In 1979 Carole Marsh was named Communicator of the Year for her corporate communications work with major national and international corporations.

   Marsh is the founder and CEO of Gallopade International, established in 1979. Today, Gallopade International is widely recognized as a leading source of educational materials for every state and many countries. Marsh and Gallopade were recipients of the 2004 Teachers' Choice Award. Marsh has written more than 50 Carole Marsh Mysteries™. In 2007, she was named Georgia Author of the Year. Years ago, her children, Michele and Michael, were the original characters in her mystery books. Today, they continue the Carole Marsh Books tradition by working at Gallopade. By adding grandchildren Grant and Christina as new mystery characters, she has continued the tradition for a third generation.

   Ms. Marsh welcomes correspondence from her readers. You can e-mail her at fanclub@gallopade.com, visit carolemarshmysteries.com, or write to her in care of Gallopade International, P.O. Box 2779, Peachtree City, Georgia, 30269 USA.

Built-In Book Club
Talk About It!

1. Who was your favorite character? Why?

2. If you were a slave, would you risk your life to take the Underground Railroad? Why or why not?

3. How would it feel to have your family split apart?

4. What was the scariest part of the book? Why?

5. The slave states and free states are listed on page 36. Was your state a slave state or a free state? Why did slaves   in Texas go to Ohio, Michigan, Indiana, or Illinois instead of going to Canada or Delaware?

6. What were some ways that slaves passed along messages? Do you know why slaves did not use written messages?

7. The kids were very dependent on the kindness of people they didn't really know. Can you remember all the times people helped them?

8. What was your favorite part of the book? Why?

Built-In Book Club
Bring It To Life!

1. Make a timeline! Track every place the children go during their Underground Railroad journey and make a timeline. Add pictures to show what was happening!

2. Find a map of the United States. Label the states that were free states, and the states that were slave states (see page 36). Outline the free states green, and the slave states red.

3. Make a quilt! Gather quilt materials including cotton batting, white fabric, colored fabric, fabric scraps, buttons, embroidery thread, needles, thread, yarn, ribbon, and sewing scissors.

    *   Create a design for your quilt on paper.
    *   Cut nine squares each of the white fabric and colored fabric. The white ones will be used for backing.
    *   Create your design on the colored squares. Use buttons, fabric scraps, yarn, etc.
    *   When a quilt piece is finished, lay it on a backing piece and sew three sides together.
    *   Stuff the piece with cotton batting, and sew the fourth side closed.
    *   Sew all nine pieces together to form your quilt. Add a fabric border if you want!
    *   Embroider club members' initials and the date in the corner. You are finished!

UNDERGROUND RAILROAD

Places To Go & Things To Know!

Tubman African American Museum, Macon, Georgia – museum features 14 galleries of exhibits, a beautiful mural, and several traveling exhibitions

Underground Railroad Museum, Flushing, Ohio – exhibits show the American culture of slavery, the abolitionist movement, and the Underground Railroad in Ohio; also features collection of related publications

National Underground Railroad Museum, Maysville, Kentucky – featuring artifacts and exhibits, the museum sits near a central escape route on the banks of the Ohio River used by fugitive slaves; location is surrounded by Underground Railroad "stations" and historic homes of "conductors"

Hubbard House Underground Railroad Museum, Ashtabula, Ohio – historic restored home of Ohio abolitionist William Hubbard who harbored numerous runaway slaves on their way to Canada

William Still Underground Railroad Foundation – dedicated to educating people about Underground Rail Road history

The National Underground Railroad Family Reunion Festival, Philadelphia, Pennsylvania – annual three-day public event created to reunite the descendants of those involved with the Underground Railroad

New Castle Court House Museum, New Castle, Delaware – Underground Railroad exhibit features information about one of Delaware's most prominent abolitionists, Thomas Garrett

Harriet Tubman Museum, Cambridge, Maryland – museum and birthplace of Harriet Tubman

National Underground Railroad Freedom Center, Cincinnati, Ohio – national interactive learning center includes exhibits about Cincinnati's "Freedom Corridor" escape route between Maysville, Kentucky and Madison, Indiana

Buxton National Historic Site and Museum, North Buxton, Ontario, Canada – museum about Canada's role in the Underground Railroad; a haven of freedom for fugitive slaves escaping North

National Museum for American History, Washington, D.C. – located on the National Mall, museum features hands-on exhibits, lecture series, festivals, and musical performances.

African American Museum, Philadelphia, Pennsylvania – located in the historic district, established in 1976 to interpret African American life and culture

National Constitution Center, Philadelphia, Pennsylvania – first museum in the world dedicated to the U.S. Constitution; features more than 100 interactive exhibits; located on Independence Mall.

Library Hall, Philadelphia, Pennsylvania – predecessor to the Library of Congress; in 1789, became the first library open to the public; features rare manuscripts including the original journals of the Lewis and Clark expedition, first editions of Sir Isaac Newton's *Principia* and Charles Darwin's *Origin of Species*, and the Declaration of Independence in Thomas Jefferson's own handwriting

Independence Hall, Philadelphia, Pennsylvania – once known as the Pennsylvania State House, built in the 1700s; site where representatives from the original 13 colonies debated, drafted, adopted, and signed the Declaration of Independence

Liberty Bell Pavilion, Philadelphia, Pennsylvania – bell rang from the tower of Independence Hall to call citizens to hear the first public reading of the Declaration of Independence in 1776; Liberty Bell Pavilion opened in 1976 in anticipation of America's bicentennial celebration and the new Liberty Bell Center will open in October 2003; each Fourth of July the bell is rung in unison with thousands of bells across America

Bethel African Methodist Episcopal Church, Lancaster, Pennsylvania – reenactment production of the Underground Railroad includes monologues by "conductors" and "passengers"

USS Constellation, Baltimore, Maryland – only Civil War vessel still afloat, sits in the Inner Harbor; last all-sail warship built by the U.S. Navy

Betsy Ross House, Philadelphia, Pennsylvania – historic landmark features artifacts, furniture, and gift shop that only sells American-made merchandise

The African American Odyssey, Washington, D.C. – exhibit of African American history located in the Library of Congress

City Hall, Philadelphia, Pennsylvania – historic government building located in the center of Philadelphia, statue of William Penn sits atop tower

Harriet Tubman Home, Auburn, New York – home where Harriet's parents relocated from Canada

Harriet Tubman Home for the Aged, Auburn, New York – house that Harriet called her last work, now a museum

National Women's Hall of Fame, Seneca Falls, New York – honored Harriet Tubman by inducting her posthumously into the Hall

Baltimore Aquarium, Baltimore, Maryland – houses more than 10,500 marine and freshwater animals in its exhibits and facilities; the main aquarium building holds more than one million gallons of water!

GLOSSARY

abolitionist: a person who thinks slavery is wrong and works to stop it

conductor: a member of the Underground Railroad who led slaves to safety in the North or Canada

drinking gourd: code for the North Star (Polaris) which lies almost directly north in the sky

droned: talked in a boring voice

gauge: an instrument for measuring

intriguing: arousing interest or curiosity

johnnycake: bread or cake made of cornmeal and water or milk; also called cornpone and cornbread

pavilion: an open structure for temporary shelter

perplexed: confused

plantation: a large farm; usually where rice, tobacco or cotton was grown

rendezvous: a prearranged place of meeting

scrapple: mixture of cornmeal mush, meat, and herbs – shaped into loaves and sliced for frying

stations: homes and barns where slaves escaping to the North could hide safely

stationmaster: person in charge of a hiding place

travelers: runaway slaves; also called freight, dry goods, packages, and hardware

SAT **virtual:** something that represents the real thing but is not real

Underground Railroad: a group of people who helped slaves escape to freedom

SCAVENGER HUNT!

Recipe for fun: Read the book, take the tour, find the items on this list, and check them off! (Hint: Look high and low!!) *Teachers: you have permission to reproduce this form for your students.*

__1. William Penn

__2. red whistle

__3. Liberty Bell

__4. magic lamp

__5. johnnycake

__6. symbol of freedom

__7. quilt or quilt square

__8. page in a journal

__9. gourd

__10. any Pennsylvania food

WRITE YOUR OWN MYSTERY!

Make up a dramatic title!

You can pick four real kid characters!

Select a real place for the story's setting!

Try writing your first draft!

Edit your first draft!

Read your final draft aloud!

You can add art, photos or illustrations!

Share your book with others and send me a copy!

Six Secret Writing Tips from Carole Marsh!

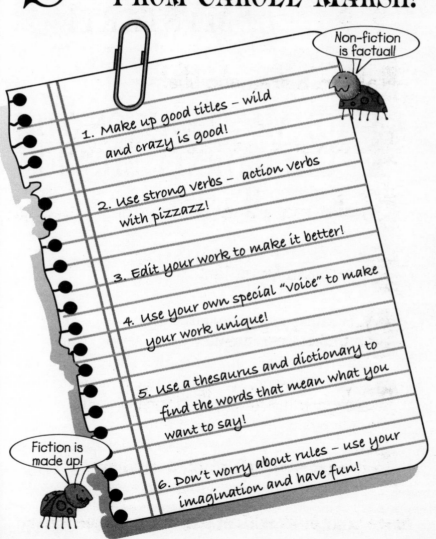

Non-fiction is factual!

1. Make up good titles – wild and crazy is good!

2. Use strong verbs – action verbs with pizzazz!

3. Edit your work to make it better!

4. Use your own special "voice" to make your work unique!

5. Use a thesaurus and dictionary to find the words that mean what you want to say!

Fiction is made up!

6. Don't worry about rules – use your imagination and have fun!

Enjoy this exciting excerpt from

THE MYSTERY ON THE CALIFORNIA MISSION TRAIL

1 A NEW MYSTERY

Christina and Grant stared at the black and white pieces of the chess game they were playing. Christina's hand hovered just inches over the board while they motionlessly listened to Mimi's phone conversation. "California missions? Mystery? Sounds exciting! We'll fly out immediately," they heard Mimi say.

Christina Yother, 9, a fourth-grader in Peachtree City, and her brother Grant, 7, ran into the kitchen where their grandmother Mimi had just hung up the phone. The smell of fudgy brownies filled the air. "Where Mimi? Where are we going this time?" Christina asked, looking up expectantly.

"What?" asked Mimi, looking at her grandchildren with a smile. "You two weren't eavesdropping again, were you?"

Grant and Christina tried to look apologetic, but their bright blue eyes quickly went back to excited anticipation of where they might be going.

"We're going to California," said Mimi, "and we've got to leave tomorrow. My mission mystery has to be written by July."

Grant looked at Christina and shrugged his shoulders. They were both used to Mimi's indecipherable comments. Their grandmother was not like any of the other grandmothers they knew. She had bright blond hair, wrote mystery books, and took off on adventures at a moment's notice. The best part was she always took them along too!

"What's your mission, Mimi?" asked Grant.

"What?" asked Mimi, as she rubbed Grant's short blond hair in confusion. "Oh, not my mission—California missions! In the 1700s and 1800s, Spanish padres, or priests, established a chain of 21 missions stretching along the California coast for 600 miles. The missions are churches, but they're also more. In addition to the church, missions included living quarters for the padres and the Indians they converted to Christianity, plus everything they needed to survive."

"Mission grounds included irrigated fields

planted with grains, vineyards, stables, herds of cattle and sheep, and gardens," she continued. "Today, the missions are open to visitors who come to tour the restored buildings and view the ancient artifacts, golden statues, and elaborate altars. Missions are an important part of California's history."

"Why are we going to see them?" Christina asked.

"The California missions are the setting for my next mystery book," Mimi replied. "The old adobe and stone buildings with all their Spanish arches and orange tile roofs will be a great backdrop to some scary adventures!"

Grant looked up at Mimi with a grin. "Maybeee there's gold in them thar hills!" he exclaimed.

"Oh brother," said Christina, rolling her eyes. She was used to Grant's silly sayings and songs. In fact, she had plenty of her own. Obviously he knew California was famous for the Gold Rush. He had always been interested in any kind of search for treasure!

"How long will we be there, Mimi?" Christina asked in her most serious and mature voice.

"That depends on how long it takes to solve the mystery," Mimi answered mysteriously.

"Uh, oh," Christina thought. Mimi made that sound so easy. But Christina recalled all the spooky trouble that Mimi could get them all into on any of her mystery book writing adventures–or misadventures, as Christina preferred to call them.